D1527082

THE BLACK WOLF

by GALAD ELFLANDSSON

. . . written with the care and concepts . . .
of a Lovecraft . . .
the record of weird events and
monstrous worship from colonial times
to the present — events which culminate
in strikingly vivid action
and great horror.

Illustrated by Randy Broecker

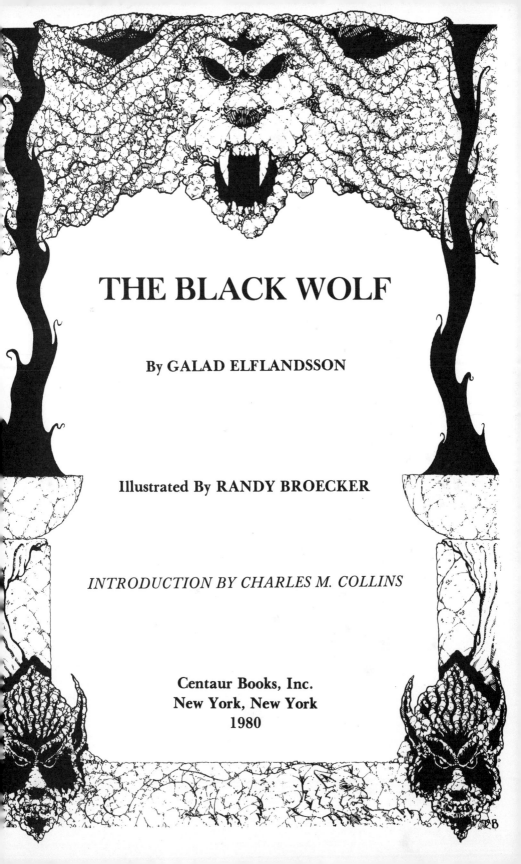

THE BLACK WOLF

By **GALAD ELFLANDSSON**

Illustrated By **RANDY BROECKER**

INTRODUCTION BY CHARLES M. COLLINS

Centaur Books, Inc.
New York, New York
1980

THE BLACK WOLF
Copyright © 1979 by Galad Elflandsson
Illustrations copyright © 1979 by Randy Broecker

Centaur Books edition — first published 1980

Printed in the United States of America

ISBN 0-87818-015-X

Distributed by
Como Sales, Inc.
799 Broadway, New York, N.Y. 10003

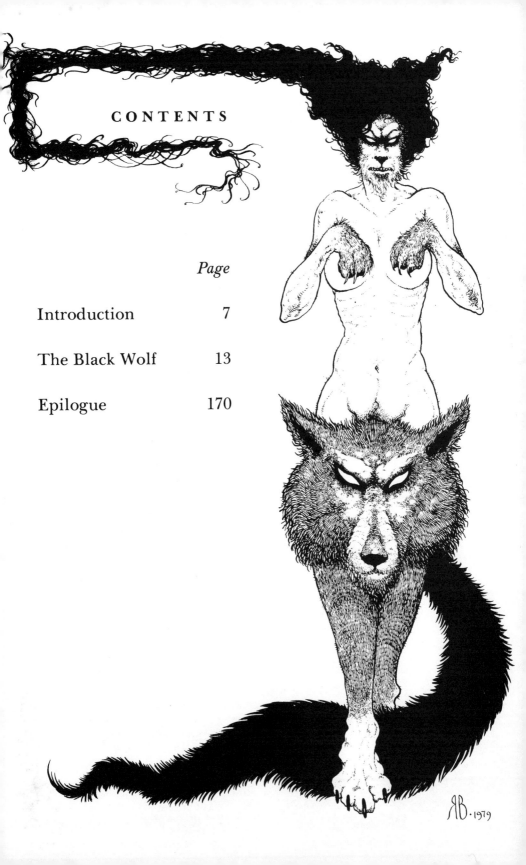

CONTENTS

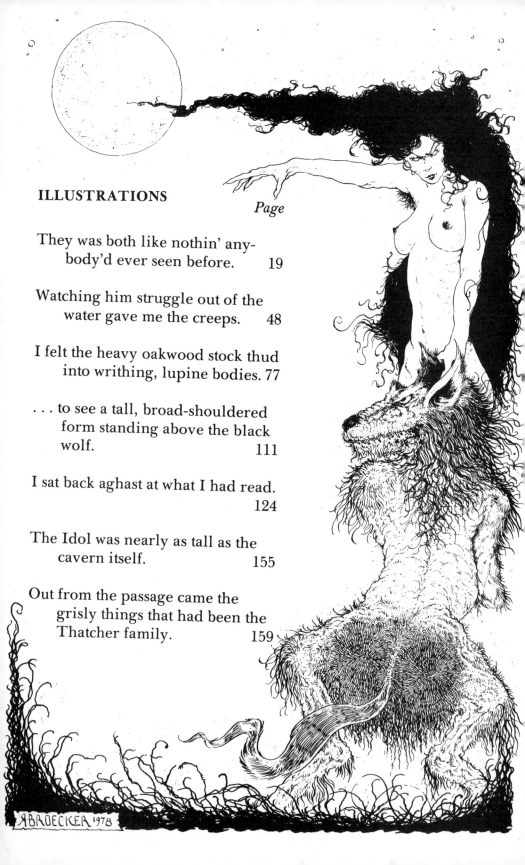

ILLUSTRATIONS

RBROECKER 1978

INTRODUCTION

Galad Elflandsson, Rhode Island, and that legendary volume of unspeakable horrors, THE KING IN YELLOW, are now as interrelated in my mind as are Ambrose Bierce, Carcosa, and Robert W. Chambers. Admittedly a wholly subjective connection, but a few words of explanation will, hopefully, introduce a rather extraordinary young man with a very extraordinary talent.

My first contact with Galad Elflandsson occurred about a year ago during a visit with publisher Donald M. Grant in West Kingston, Rhode Island. Grant had recently finished reading an original manuscript submitted by a young writer currently residing in Ottawa, Ontario. He was impressed with the work — a collection of stories entitled THE EXILE & OTHER TALES OF CARCOSA. "I think you'll like this, Charles," he said with a twinkle in his eye, as he passed me a bulky packet. "Who is he?" I asked, noting the rather unusual by-line. "I've never heard of him." "You will," I was assured. "He's going to be one of the big names in fantasy someday."

Several days later, back at my home in New York, I began reading the title story. It was late in the evening, but I decided to finish one piece before retiring — just to get an idea of this writer's style, I thought. And then I became caught up in Galad Elflandsson's special magic. It was my undoing for that night! I understood that gleam in Donald Grant's eye when he passed me the manuscript.

He knew I would become hooked from the very first page.

But what a rare and wonderful experience to discover someone, a newcomer, totally unknown, who can fashion prose that is a pure joy to read, and create a narrative so gripping, so compelling, that one is virtually impelled to turn the next page.

In THE EXILE & OTHER TALES OF CARCOSA, Elflandsson perpetuates that small but fascinating canon of horror which began with Ambrose Bierce, was developed by Robert W. Chambers, and which later inspired such outstanding chroniclers of weird tales as H. P. Lovecraft and August Derleth. Galad Elflandsson can well qualify as a candidate to this horror hall of fame. Often, too, he succeeds in transcending the strictly 'weird' genre by infusing into his creations an all-pervading fear and psychological disorientation somewhat akin to the most frightening tales of Franz Kafka.

But let us turn to THE BLACK WOLF. This was originally a novella in the Carcosa collection entitled "The Cave of the Hill Giant," and, as such, related to the sinister Bierce-Chambers mythos. Grant's interest and suggestion to expand the work to novel length started Galad into extensive revisions. Now removed from the Carcosa content of THE EXILE, the Bierce-Chambers background was replaced with a more Lovecraftian concept. Interestingly enough, I discovered that both approaches worked — worked well, as a matter of fact. The basic plot has not changed substantially, but along with the shift in literary framework, Galad has added new scenes of strikingly vivid action and horror — a feast lies just ahead.

Who is this young, talented man with a name evoking an adventurer from some ancient Scandinavian legend? Eventually, after I had been invited to do this introduction, Galad provided me with a few pages of biographical information. And later I was to have the pleasure of meeting Galad and his charming and supportive wife, Teena, during their recent visit to New York. The precise and exacting quality of his writing style had led me to envision a somewhat academic and sophisticated personage behind the name, while the story themes tempted me to suspect a touch of decadence. Instead, I met a genuinely warm and unassuming young man, bearded, informal, and possessing a spirit of conviviality that would make any Norse hero proud.

He was born in New York City on November 22, 1951, and admits to a rather solitary childhood and adolescence. He resided briefly in Miami, Boston, and Los Angeles, working in such diverse fields as finance, land sales, woodwork, and commercial, residential, and industrial painting. He wrote his first story at twenty-three, and met Teena soon after. They were married in 1976, settled in Montreal, but presently live in Ottawa.

He was introduced to fantastic literature at age ten when he discovered the novels of Edgar Rice Burroughs. Some eight or nine years later he would encounter new literary realms in the heroic fantasy which then proliferated the market. He was totally converted by the Ballantine Adult Fantasy Series, and he now tries to read at least one book every two days. His primary interest is in fantasy and the Norse sagas, although he does admit to reading some of the historical romances of Dumas and Edison Marshall, with occasional departures to Sherlock Holmes, Ellery Queen, and Agatha Christie.

His first appearance in print was the January, 1977, issue of *Dark Fantasy*, published by Gene Day. Since then his work has seen publication in *Copper Toadstool, Beyond the Fields We Know, Dragonbane, Nightshade,* and *Heroic Fantasy.*

Galad Elflandsson — an extraordinary name; an extraordinary talent. I believe publication of THE BLACK WOLF is a major event. This is but the beginning. I am extremely honored to be a small part of this beginning, because I cannot but concur with Donald Grant's judgment: "He is going to be one of the big names in fantasy someday."

And now a rare treat awaits you, and the experience may well be just as formidable as was your first encounter with Poe, Machen, Robert Chambers, or H. P. Lovecraft.

Charles M. Collins
July, 1979

ONE

"It's easy for you to shrug when you hear my name and say, 'Corey Thatcher is mad.' It's easy for you to dismiss all the things I've said as the ravings of a lunatic. I've lived apart from you for precisely those reasons; because you're all careless, unfeeling people who prefer to hold my family's past against me rather than let my warnings upset the balance of your smug, well-ordered lives. But I'm not mad and I'm warning you this one last time to leave Thatcher's Ferry. If you refuse to heed my warning, then you'll learn at first hand that I was right. You'll wish that you had listened, but by then it will be too late! You'll see! Just wait and you *will* see!"

With those words, Corwin Thatcher harangued the good people of Thatcher's Ferry on the summer afternoon of June 18, 19— —. He stood on the wooden steps of Daley's General Store, a livid bruise swelling on his bearded cheek where an apple, presumably thrown by a mischievous child of the village, had struck him. His bag of groceries lay torn and scattered in the dust and observing the curious spectacle of his anger from across the street, I had to admit that his behaviour seemed a great deal more like that of a madman than anything else. No sooner had the missile found its mark then he had literally thrown the paper bag from himself to stand rigidly glaring in the direction from whence the attack had come. Failing to find the culprit, he proceeded to work himself into a frothing rage, tearing at the long, shaggy mass of his grizzled hair and bellowing like a wounded bull. His small, close-set eyes seemed to blaze with a dreadful light, and beneath the shadow of his whiskered upper lip, he actually ground his teeth until blood oozed from his mouth into the tangle of his beard.

It was a Saturday. I had been fishing nearby for almost a week, finally realizing the much-needed and long-awaited vacation I had planned for over a year. I had come into Thatcher's Ferry to replace a screw that had loosened from my reel at the sporting shop owned by Calvin Adderley. I had been there before, just after arriving in the area, to pick up a spool of line, but my first visit had been a lot less interesting than this one promised to be. The village was crowded with farmers from the surrounding countryside as the fuming giant clad in a checkered flannel shirt and faded denims grew louder in his remonstrations. Most of them drew their families closer, to listen and watch with wide grins on their weatherbeaten faces. Scarcely believing that such anger could result from such a harmless prank as the throwing of an apple, I must confess that I, too, gazed at Corwin Thatcher with some amusement. When his tirade was over and he had stalked to his battered station-wagon and driven off, I found that Calvin Adderley had joined me on the porch of his store and was also smiling broadly.

"How's the fishin', Mr. Damon?" he said, turning to me. "Catch anythin' worth talkin' about?"

"Nothing to speak of, really," I replied to his still smiling face. "But it's the relaxation that I wanted more than anything else and if the fish don't feel like biting, I won't be too upset."

"True enough about the relaxin' part," he nodded. "You city folks seem t'have a need t'go elsewhere fer that sorta thing. You ever seen the likes o' mad Thatcher in the city?"

"No, I can't say that I have," I said, shaking my head. "I've seen some awfully off-beat characters get worked up about all sorts of things . . . but he's taken the prize for my money, Mr. Adderley."

Adderley grinned, splitting his thin, spectacled face almost in two in the process of doing so.

"Calvin's the name. Cal is better. That's what

most people say when they meet up with Corey Thatcher fer the first time."

"Who is he . . . Cal?" I asked, my curiosity piqued by his conversation. "And what was all his talk about warnings and the like?"

"Really wanna know?" he said, cocking his head to one side and eyeing me expectantly.

"Well . . . I do need a replacement screw for my reel. Why don't you tell me about him inside. I'm afraid that I really would like to know more about this 'mad Thatcher' of yours."

"Yep. Most city folks do," he grinned again. "He's a bit of a celebrity with some o' the folks that come up here regular. Been rantin' and ravin' bout one thing or another fer years. Come on then. I'll tell ya all about him and throw in a cold bottle o' pop, too,"

I followed the lanky owner into his shop, welcoming the cool semi-darkness after the suffocating heat outside. Calvin Adderley's store was perhaps the most modern of all the stores in Thatcher's Ferry. His walls were hung with just about anything a sportsman in the back woods could ask for, not to mention the three, spotless glass counters that rimmed the walls of the store. Calvin Adderley was a pure rustic sort, but one who had enough business sense to know that in an

isolated region of wood and stream, there were bound
to be hunters and fishermen who would have unexpected needs. Adderley filled those needs, all the
little extras that made sporting a more intricate pastime
than it had ever been in the past. He cleared a small
space on one of his display tables, drew up a pair of
canvas deck-chairs and went off to find two bottles of
"pop," as he called it.

"Here ya are," he said with a broad sweep of his
hand toward the table. "Sit yerself right down and I'll
give ya the earful, though by now ya must've made the
connection 'tween Corey Thatcher and Thatcher's
Ferry. . . ."

The connection had occurred to me and I took
the frosty bottle from him gratefully, settling down
into my chair with an avid interest.

"Well . . . it's a long story," began Adderley, "but
it's a good 'un cause I sure as heck told it enough times
and ain't no one ever been bored with it. Corey's
great-great-grandfather was Captain Elias Thatcher
round about 1775 or so; leastwise, that was when he
first showed up in these parts. He was a sailor, travelled
all over the place and made a heap o' money doin' it
too, cause Corey still comes into town and spends gold
pieces that are a hundred and seventy-five years old.

Anyways, Captain Thatcher come up here into these parts lookin' t'settle down and he brought his wife along with him, Kerinna was her name, or somethin' close t'that. They was both like nothin' anybody'd ever seen before; him bein' big as a horse and every bit as strong, all whiskered and wearin' his captain's coat. A lot like Corey, I suppose. She was said t'be a foreigner from some place like Arabia, a real good lookin' one though her skin was all pasty-white and her hair was black as midnight with big, black eyes that could scare the breath right outta a hungry she-bear if she took t'starin' at the beast fer too long.

"They come up right when things was gettin' hot all over with the British. The Revolution, Independence Day and all that. Captain Elias went round with his gold pieces sayin' t'all them that lived hereabouts then that with war comin' on fer certain, it would be best if they all got moved in a bit closer t'each other fer protection; that he'd make it worth their whiles t'give up their farms and move into the town here that he was gonna build for 'em. Some said 'Sure thing' when they seen the colour of his money. Others said 'Sure thing' when Kerinna Thatcher came round and eyed 'em all up just a little bit. So Captain Elias ended up with half the land here to himself and everyone else

got his gold and came t'live in his town, runnin' the
ferry that used t'cross the creek on the other side o' the
Bishop house or workin' fer the Captain himself —
buildin' this or that fer him or tendin' t'all the livestock
that was his now. Some folks went t'work on the farms
that hadn't been sold t'the Captain.

"Then the war come along and don't ya know that
nobody ever did see a red coat or a blue one either fer
the whole time. There was some grumblin', some that
was thinkin' that Elias had taken 'em fer their farms . . .
but life waren't so bad and Thatcher went on payin'
his wages in good gold so everybody was satisfied in
the end. It waren't till the rumours started goin' bout
his wife that folks took on definite dislike fer the both
of 'em, and when the Captain offered more gold fer
anyone who'd help him t'build a house out in the
woods, folks jumped to it just t'get him and his Kerinna
outta town."

"What kinda of rumours, Calvin?" I asked on cue.
I felt pretty sure that Calvin had told that part of the
story in exactly the same way for years . . . and had
been asked the same question each time. He grinned
appreciably.

"Thought ya might be interested. Just when the
war was gettin' started, seems there was two people

disappeared from the town without a trace — a woman and then a small boy. And before that, folks that hadn't sold their farms kept findin' their herds all torn up by wolves come mysterious-like into the county. They said it was Kerinna's doin', 'specially since people'd wander out t'the Thatcher house after it was built just t'spy on 'em . . . and they'd come back with stories o' lights burnin' at all hours whether the Thatchers was home or not, odd noises comin' from the attic and wolves hangin' round the house like they was waitin' t'be fed or somethin'. Them stories went on fer a long time, but after the war came news that Kerinna had birthed the Captain a son, Jeremiah Thatcher. Six years later or so, a couple on the edge o' town got all torn up when a pack o' wolves tried t'runn off with their four-year old daughter. Rumours started flyin' thicker'n locusts at drought-time and it woulda gone bad fer the Thatchers then if not fer the fire that burned their house t'the ground with Captain Elias in it. At any rate, after that they got left alone and 'Witch' Thatcher (that's what folks had started callin' her), along with little Jeremiah, buried the Captain in the cemetery just down the street here and lived on in an old shed they'd had built near the house."

Adderley paused in his story to wait on a local customer who had walked in and had been listening with a smile on his face for a few minutes. It was rather obvious that he had heard Calvin's rendition of the Thatcher family history before, probably under similar circumstances. Oddly enough, I had begun to sympathise with Corey Thatcher. Crazy or not, everyone seemed to think he was a joke, a clown for the amusement of the rest of the town . . . and I could not help feeling that his erratic behaviour towards these people might well be justified. While lost in this thought, Calvin Adderley came back to our table to resume his tale.

"Let's see now, where was I?" he said, scratching his head. "Elias, the fire . . . now I got it. After the Captain died, things got quiet fer fifteen years or so. More stories bout 'Witch' Thatcher got told but they was just stories fer all anybody knew and soon as ya please, Jeremiah was all grown up and married to a girl named Catherine Fletcher, the daughter of his dead father's first mate come all the way from Boston t'marry young Jeremy. Then the house got rebuilt just t'where it stands today, not far from where ya say yer campin', as a matter o' fact. Jeremy and his new bride moved in there along with his mother . . . and that's when the stories got t'their worst and all the bad feelin's fer them folks rose up t'good, honest hate."

"Jeremiah was every bit as queer as his mother?" I interjected hastily. Calvin shook his head vehemently in reply.

"Nope. Jeremiah and his Catherine was good people, goin' outta their way t'be friendly and helpful t'everyone in town — but it was his mother that caused all the trouble and not him. When Catherine gave birth to Tobias (that was Corey's grandfather) in 1825, 'Witch' Thatcher just sorta went crackers, took t'wanderin' all over and scarin' the heck outta man and farm beast alike. The tales got told how she'd have bears and wolves followin' her around in the woods at night; how she'd be out there till dawn, shriekin' and brewin' up hell-fire in a cauldron. Wolves started chewin' up the cattle again, too; of course, she was the one t'get blamed fer it. The long and short was that Tobias grew up lookin' and actin' just like his grandma.

"About the time he was fourteen or so, neighbourin' farmers started complainin' that their livestock was bein' stolen off night after night, findin' 'em the next mornin' all butchered up and half-eaten. Then it was that kind old Jeremiah Thatcher roused everybody fer a huntin' party t'kill off the wolves. I guess he sorta felt that by leadin' the hunt he was makin' up fer all the stories about his mother. Anyway, early one mornin' they went off into the hills t'rout 'em out. Tobias went along, aimin' t'bag himself a couple o' wolves with a bow and arrows that he'd carved fer himself. Sure enough, they come back that night with Toby cryin' and nothin' t'show fer anybody's troubles but the body o' Jeremy Thatcher . . . with one of his son's crooked arrows in his head where Toby'd shot him by mistake, thinkin' he was a wolf. A week later, Catherine comes runnin' into town completely outta her head and screamin' that Toby done shot his father on purpose. That didn't go on fer long, though. Her brother came t'fetch her back t'Boston and the last anybody ever heard o' poor Catherine, she was babblin' away in a lunatic house there.

"Tobias and his grandma went on livin' in the house all alone, him growin' up and roamin' over the countryside with a weird look in his eyes just like the one folks seen in Kerinna when she and the Captain first come along. Waren't no doubt about it then. Toby was goin' outta his head, too . . . except that people swore it waren't over killin' his father cause he'd have this twisted sorta smile whenever anybody's mention it t'him, which waren't too often since most was goin' outta their way t'avoid the Thatchers by that time.

"Anyway, Toby started hangin' round what used t'be the Tanner house, gogglin' at Amy Tanner each time she'd step out the door. Course she was a bit slow, what ya'd call retarded nowadays . . . but it was nothin' but her big . . . well, ya know what I mean . . . that Toby wanted, and since she waren't much more than a drag on her parents (who wasn't too well off t'begin with), they was glad when Toby got bothered enough t'steal her one day and marry her. Was common knowledge that the preacher who done the ceremony swore t'his dyin' day that Toby had all but undressed poor Amy 'fore he even finished with his 'I do's . . . but that's just a bitta colour t'the story. Want another pop, Mr. Damon? Or are ya tired o'listenin' t'stories bout crazy Corey's kin?"

"No, not at all," I answered enthusiastically. "You tell a marvelous story and you've got me caught up in it. It's just that it's all a bit beyond my experience. I'm city folk, as you say."

"I didn't mean any insult, Mr. Damon," said Cal hurriedly. "City folk have got t'get away from the city once in a while and when they do, often as not, I stand t'profit by it. But I try t'make their gettin' away pleasant, ya know what I mean? Y'have t'realize that some country folk ought t'get away from the country. Me, I'm happy. But there's others who ain't so happy and it can get mighty lonesome out here. It does strange things t'the unhappy ones . . . like the Thatchers. They just went on makin' things worse fer themselves . . . like Toby marryin' half-wit Amy, fer instance. Here's yer pop.

　　"But gettin' back t'where I was, Toby took t'draggin' Amy round with him whenever he'd go on them jaunts through the hills. For years and years, nigh on thirty, it went on like that and people began to wonder if a new Thatcher would ever come along and what kinda Thatcher he'd be with Toby and Amy fer parentage (See, everybody got t'expectin' nothin' but sons from the Thatchers and dang me if that's all they ever did have). Reason they wondered was because Toby didn't take no particular care about where he took his pleasure of Amy and plenty said they seen the two of 'em naked as the day they was born, runnin' through the hills. I heard tell they even got surprised in the cemetery one night! Meanwhile, old grandma 'Witch' Thatcher was pushin' at least a hundred and ten. Course nobody'd seen her much fer a while, but come 1866, Toby buried her next t'the Captain and there waren't a soul who knew somethin' 'bout the old days who was sorry t'see her go.

"Well, at that point, there was a few new families in town here and it'd grown just a bit larger. With 'Witch' Thatcher in her grave, stories about her tailed off and folks breathed easier . . . but Thatcher means 'surprises' and the biggest surprise of 'em all came five years later in 1871 when Amy, who was a couple o' years older than Toby t'start with, came into town pregnant as a cow at age forty-nine. Waren't much left o' her, truly. Toby had run that poor soul ragged and when Amory Thatcher was born, she died givin' birth t'him.

"Amory was screwy from the word GO. About the time he was seven years old, Tobias took him fishin' on the lake, same one yer fishin', and never came back — he fell outta their boat and drowned. After that, Amory just wandered around aimless, livin' like an animal what with no one t'look after him and stirrin' all sortsa trouble like stealin' chickens, killin' sheep and pokin' his nose into other folks winders at night. Mind ya, he was still livin' in the Thatcher house, but a few kids at that time sneaked up there when they knew Amory waren't around and they came back sayin' that the whole place smelled like a barn and looked twice as bad.

"Like I mentioned before, some new folks had settled into town and one of 'em was a woman by the name o' Sarah Patterson. Some swore she looked exactly like Kerinna Thatcher was said t'have looked with her eyes and all. T'tell ya the truth, I remember seein' her once when I was real young and she got angry at us kids fer playin' round her house. Scared the heck outta us, too, when she started starin'. We was glad when she moved out from town and in with Amory Thatcher. Figgered they'd both be suited real well fer each other. That was in 1905 and two years later came bastard Corey cause they never did get married.

"Even though I laugh at him, I guess he's got every reason t'be as crazy as his father. Middle o' the First World War it was, he bein' thirteen or fourteen at the time, Amory came into town drunk as a skunk and bustin' up anythin' he could lay his hands on. Folks got all riled up, my mom and dad as well, and they chased him all the way back t'his house and stood there debatin' on whether or not they should haul him out and make him pay fer all the damage he done. Surprise again! Old Amory fooled 'em. All of a sudden the attic shutters go bangin' out and there he stands with dark-haired Sarah on one hand and Corey shiverin' on the other. Next thing ya know he's pulled out this big knife and cut her throat from ear t'ear, laughin' all the while he's kickin' her bleedin' out the winder. Probably woulda done the same t'Corey if Larry Hanson, God rest him cause it drove him crazy too, hadn't picked up his rifle and put a bullet in Amory's chest.

"That was the end of it, Mr. Damon. They never found Tobias's body in the lake but all the other Thatchers is buried in the cemetery not a thousand yards from where yer sittin'. All of 'em 'cept Catherine Fletcher, who died back in Boston, and Corey himself. When he got a bit older, he took off fer almost ten years. Rumour had it he went through some New England college and then travelled a lot. Guess he was tryin' t'forget all the strangeness in him . . . but it didn't do him much good after all. Truth is, Corey ain't half so bad fer a Thatcher; but heck! That bunch has been this town's only source o' entertainin' from the beginnin'. Compared t'his back relations, he's as sober as the Pope . . . but us folks got into grinnin' at the Thatcher doin's a long way back and it's hard t'break the habit.

"Corey's kept t'himself and his woods mostly. Only comes into town t'buy shells fer his shotgun and

groceries fer his belly. Maybe we been too hard on
him, but lately he's shown us them Thatcher antics in
as good a style as Tobias or Amory before him."

Calvin Adderley pushed his chair back from the
table and gathered up our empty soda bottles. The
good-natured, good-humored smiles with which he
had recounted Corey Thatcher's ancestry were suddenly gone from his face and a noticeable pallour had
replaced them.

"It's quite a story, Calvin," I said, rising uncomfortably to stretch my legs. "Hardly the kind of story
one would expect to hear in such beautiful, unspoiled
country."

"I guess it does take somethin' outta ya," he said
with a sickly attempt at a smile. "Don't know why I tell
it over and over again like I do. It sorta creeps up on
ya after ya've gone through it as much as I have. Hope
ya enjoyed it, anyway."

"I don't know that 'enjoy' is the right word for it,"
I said, forcing a laugh. "It was certainly interesting . . .
but what has Corey Thatcher done lately? What was
he talking about this afternoon? I don't mean to pry.
It's just that you've made me curious."

Adderley was silent. He shuffled around his store
for a few minutes, inspecting the glass counters and
looking incredibly drained when I thought of the

ebullience with which he had greeted me earlier on his porch.

"Please don't bother if you'd rather not," I said with some concern. "You've already indulged my inquisitive nature too much."

"Heck. Don't worry about it, Mr. Damon. Course I'll tell ya. Like I said, the Thatchers just get t'ya after a while, that's all.

"What Corey's been talkin' about is just more craziness. Round Christmas time livestock started disappearin' again like in my story and a few wolves showed up in these parts, too . . . so Corey's been rantin' and ravin' that we're all in a lotta danger livin' here; that we all oughta pick up and scoot cause somethin' terrible's gonna happen real soon. He never tells us what's gonna happen and he never tells us why. All he says is that the wolves and the livestock bein' carried off and killed is part of it, the beginnin'. It's gotten t'be a fixation with him. He's gotten louder and louder and louder about it since December as well as throwin' an occasional trantrum or two like the one this afternoon. Heck! He's just crazy! He's a Thatcher all right and he's crazy just like the rest of 'em."

The sun was hidden in the hills when I left Calvin's store and headed back to my campsite on the lake.

Halfway there, I realized that in listening to Calvin's story, I had forgotten to get the screw for my reel that had been the original purpose of my visit to town. I was almost minded to turn my car around and make a quick trip back for it but decided otherwise when the road started to wind off onto the narrow, forest track already cloaked in the shadows of evening. Tomorrow morning would do just as well.

That night, comfortable in my sleeping bag beneath the overhanging boughs of a willow tree, I found my thoughts continually straying to the strange tale that had filled my afternoon; that, and the image of Corwin Thatcher, foaming with rage on the steps of Daley's General Store. I tried to place him in the history I had heard and found him very well-suited to have a part in it . . . in every aspect but one. The thing that kept me awake for most of the night was that I couldn't consciously put my finger on the nature of the one aspect that didn't fit.

TWO

I woke the next morning to the rustle of marsh ducks in the waving clumps of reeds that shored the lake, to the sharp tapping of woodpeckers in the forest, to the soft whistling of pheasants that seemed ever to be just beyond the capacity of my eyes to separate from the cover of thick undergrowth through which they picked their way. The air hummed, a morning breeze swept over the lake, heavy with the damp, redolent scent of the pine woods around me. Through the cascading boughs of my willow tree, the sky seemed to be one unblemished expanse of dazzling, crystalline blue. It was a rare day, a jewel in the treasure house of Nature's swift passage of days . . . but I crawled out of my sleeping bag feeling like my vacation had lost something of its lazy splendour, been darkened by the shadow of the Thatcher family's maddened history. Calvin Adderley's last remark had not rung true in my ears. It had been as if he had tried to reassure himself of Corey Thatcher's insanity. The Thatchers had gotten to him . . . and now, damn it! they had gotten to me.

I sat myself down to make a fire, brooding on Corwin Thatcher's oddness of character while the bacon began to sizzle in my fry-pan and the coffee pot intruded its plopping noises into my dejection. Even as I cursed Calvin Adderley for telling me the story, I heaped upon myself a greater abuse for the curiosity that had made me listen. The bacon burned to cinders, the eggs didn't scramble the way I liked them and the coffee tasted like I had dredged the bottom of the lake with the pot . . . and I kept on hearing Calvin's voice saying, " . . . the Thatchers get t'ya after a while, that's all . . ."

"Yes, damn it, they do!" I exclaimed aloud. "But I'm going to have my vacation in spite of them!"

Angrily, I flung the remains of my breakfast into the ashes of the fire and stamped across the clearing with the pots and pans. I knelt at the edge of the lake, scrubbing furiously, intent on going back into town, replacing the screw in my reel and coming right back for one long afternoon of fishing on the lake.

"I would vacation elsewhere if I were you."

With a start, I jumped back at the sound of the voice over my left shoulder, scrambling to my feet to face the unexpected visitor to my campsite.

"I'm Corwin Thatcher. This lake belongs to me."

It *was* Corwin Thatcher, still in his checkered

flannel shirt and ragged denims, but with a shotgun resting casually in the crook of his right arm. For a moment, I felt a thrill of fear in his presence. I was a strong six feet in height, but he towered over me by at least six inches, the bruise on his face adding a malignant cast to his features.

"I see you've heard some stories about the 'mad Thatchers,' " he said in a low voice. The bearded face bore no expression, but a note of displeasure hung in his words.

"No doubt Calvin Adderley has convinced you that I am a very dangerous lunatic who should be avoided at all costs."

He spoke with a careful precision in his speech, a quality of almost leonine assurance in his voice that bespoke intelligence and belied the charges of insanity I had heard against him.

"No. He hasn't convinced me of anything, Mr. Thatcher. Calvin Adderley is afraid of you," I answered quietly, vaguely aware that my words might very well provoke his anger. "Not because of anything in the way of personal experience, but simply because he seems to think you should be insane; that in being mad, you are nothing else frightening beyond your madness. There's something about you that scares him . . . and he tells stories in order to convince himself that you are just an ordinary, run-of-the-mill lunatic."

For an instant, he looked as if he might smile at my last statement, but he cut off its faint beginnings with a gruff reply.

"That may well be," he said a bit more kindly, "but even so, you *are* on my land and I think it would be more in your own best interests to find another spot for your fishing."

"I'm trespassing?" I asked, some of my anxiety gone in the face of his calmness. "I didn't see any signs."

"There are no signs and you are not trespassing. In the past, I have not minded anyone who fished here. Even the poor fools in Thatcher's Ferry have not found me inhospitable in that respect. I am simply saying this: You are an outsider here. I don't give a damn anymore about what happens to them . . . but this lake area has become unsafe and I will not have anyone who has no roots in this region suffering for it."

"I don't understand, Mr. Thatcher," I said, hoping I was not pressing my luck. "How is the lake unsafe?"

He did not answer immediately, but stood there

staring down at me while my heart began to pound with an annoyingly undeniable return of apprehension. This time he did smile, a cruel twist of his whiskered face as he shook his head.

"It is not for you to understand, Mr. . . .?"

"Damon," I replied, "Paul Damon. I'm a writer from the city."

"Yes . . . Mr. Damon. As I said, it is not for you to understand or question me. They jeer at me, insult me and laugh at me but I remain a considerate and hospitable man. You may stay if you wish . . . but 'Mad Corey' Thatcher has warned you against it for reasons you do not truly wish to know . . . and I shan't have any responsibility for your well-being in future."

With that, he turned and walked back into the woods, leaving me there beside the lake trembling and slack-jawed with a mixture of fear, awe and amazement. His tall form disappeared even as I watched, my ears straining to hear the expected snap of twigs and branches beneath his boots. There was nothing, nothing but the buzzing of flies, the woodpeckers tapping and the damned coo-ing of the pheasants that sounded more and more like derisive laughter to my frustrated senses. Had the whole thing been real? Had Corwin Thatcher really warned me off his property? Or was my lousy breakfast and interrupted clean-up just a dream? I looked over at my sleeping bag to make sure I wasn't still sleeping in it.

" . . . the Thatchers get t'ya after a while, that's all . . . "

I drank the dregs of my coffee pot. If I was still asleep and dreaming, I couldn't think of anything else that would jolt me awake as effectively as that.

*   *   *

When I got into town, I realized with yet another curse that it was Sunday and nothing in Thatcher's Ferry would be open except the church. It was par for the course when I considered how the day had started. I resigned myself to a day of luckless discomfort and with nothing better to do at that point, started walking down the street to the church. A tarnished brass plaque by the heavy, oakwood doors read:

> Builded bye ye goode people of Thatcher's Ferrye in ye yeare of owre Lorde, One Thousande Seven Hundred and Seventie-sixe, that ye Worde and Wisdom of He who arte owre Kynge in Heaven may not die amongst us, His children.

I smiled at the innocent faith expressed by those who had lived over a century and a half before. I wondered if the general state of the Church in our time would have shocked those earliest of Americans. Still, as I entered the church and heard the voices of the village children raised in the chanting of a hymn, I felt somewhat eased of my dreary outlook for the day and quietly took a seat in the last row of pews. I found myself quite comfortable in the musty half-light of the old house of worship.

At no great length, the services ended with the entire congregation thundering a hymn of praise to God. With much surprise, I realized that my lips were forming the words I had presumed long forgotten in my childhood and I joined my voice to the final chorus. I sang a bit louder than was necessary, I suppose, for a little girl four rows in front of me turned around and made a frowning face that I should not be so enthusiastic. I smiled at her, but that only increased the number of furrows on her little forehead and so I stopped singing altogether. Outside again, trapped in the clustering of people as they left the church, I saw Calvin, a woman who I assumed to be his wife, and a couple who I recognized as Will Daley and his wife.

"Hey there, Mr. Damon!" cried Calvin when he

saw my face in the crowd. "Been prayin' fer a bite or two?"

He and Will Daley excused themselves from their wives and walked over. They looked a bit comical together, both dressed in their Sunday suits — Calvin tall and scarecrow-thin while Will Daley's round, red face bobbed up and down at a much lesser height.

"Fergot that screw fer yer reel, ya know," grinned Calvin. He looked to have recovered from his depression of the previous evening. "Don't care how much ya pray, without that there screw t'hold things t'gether, ya won't be catchin' much in the way o' fish."

"I know," I answered sheepishly. "And I didn't realize it was Sunday until I got here."

"Don't matter at all. Come on along with Will and me. Good Lord won't be too hard on me fer fetchin' a nubbit o' hardware fer my fellow man that needs it."

"Gonna be another scorcher t'day," said Will Daley as we walked back up the street to Calvin's store. "Mighty hot fer the nineteenth o' June, though. Don't usually get weather this hot till the middle o' July."

"Well," I observed drily, "people have told me that I bring sunshine wherever I go."

"Better go easy on the bringin' then, Mr. Damon," laughed Calvin, "or all the land-grubbers round here won't have nothin' but burnt up crops t'store fer the winter and a buncha dried-up milkin' cows."

Daley and I waited on the porch of the store while he went inside to find my screw. When I mentioned to Will that Corey Thatcher had paid me a visit earlier in the morning, his eyes widened until they looked quite likely to pop right out of his round face. Calvin came out, locking the door.

"Here ya go," he said, flipping the screw at me.

"Mr. Damon here was tellin' me that 'Mad Corey' Thatcher surprised him over breakfast this mornin'," Daley informed Calvin. "He was carryin' his shotgun, too."

"Is that so?" said Adderley, raising his eyebrows. "Don't see no shot holes or bruises so I guess all ya did was talk. What'd he have t'say, Mr. Damon?"

"He said that he thought I'd be much better off if I found myself another place to do my fishing. Didn't say why when I asked him but he was very polite about the whole thing. Said I could stay if I wanted to, but that he wouldn't take the responsibility for anything that happened to me if I did."

"Hmmm," mused Calvin. "It don't do no good fer business if he's startin' in on the city folk, too. He gets stranger and stranger as the days go by."

"That ain't so strange," offered Daley. "Why last night, just 'fore I was closin' up fer the night, he was back t'get his groceries all over again."

"That ain't so strange neither, Will," said Calvin with a grin. "Crazy or no, the man's still gotta eat."

"That ain't the strange part," bubbled Daley. "Was when he come back a second time right after leavin' that was strange. Asked me if I had any sticksa dynamite lyin' 'round cause he'd like t'buy 'em from me if I did."

"Dynamite!" exclaimed Calvin. "T.N.T.?"

"Yep. That's right. Mumbled somethin' or other bout he was clearin' some tree stumps from around his house and he needed it t'clean out the roots."

"Did you have any dynamite, Mr. Daley?" I asked.

"Yep. Been sittin' in the back o' the store since I don't know when. I told him I had two dozen sticks and don't y'know he takes 'em all! Pays me with one o' his chunks o' gold and when I says I'll give him his change on a fair estimate o' what the gold was worth, he just says 'Forget it' and walks out with the case under one arm."

"Now *that* is strange, Will," said Calvin, shaking his head. "You hear anythin', Mr. Damon? His house ain't far from where yer fishin'."

I shook my head and Daley stood there rocking on his heels and looking rather pleased with himself for the "strangeness" of his bit of news. In spite of all his blustery pretensions, he was an extremely likeable fellow; but Calvin and I enjoyed a good laugh at his expense when, after a quick glance at his pocket watch, he hurried off with the most tragic expression on his face.

"Wife wants him home," snorted Calvin with amusement. "She thinks every woman in town's after her William. He's a good soul, though."

"You're not serious about his wife, are you?" I asked incredulously, watching Daley's rotund figure as it wobbled down the street.

"Sure am," he grinned back; "but listen, I told my wife Mary about ya, said ya was an all-right guy and she says t'me well why don't I ask ya over fer dinner one night seein' as ya can't be havin' much in the way o' decent food out there in the woods. So yer invited, tonight, with me and Mary at the Langdon house. Rachel Langdon is Mary's younger sister and neither one of 'em will take NO fer an answer so we'll see ya 'bout six or so and don't let no raccoons steal yer bait."

He stuck his hands in his trouser pockets and sauntered off down the street. An hour later I was in my boat, rod repaired, my line out and nothing to do but laze in the sun as it rose higher into the blue sky, blazing down with a heat so intense that the lake water seemed to boil around me. I grew drowsy, dozed three or four times and finally drifted off into the sleep I had not gotten the night before.

The sun was halfway through its western descent when a tugging on my line awakened me in time to see my rod slip over the stern of my boat and down into the water! In utter disbelief, I rubbed my eyes and stared again at the place where I had last seen it, wondering how big a fish it had taken to drag the rod out from under my leg and into the lake without a moment in between. It was the last straw, the crowning episode in my vain struggle to vacation like a normal human being. I honestly could have cried with frustration had I not been distracted by the splashing of water about halfway between my boat and the far shore of the lake.

At first, I thought it was the fish that had hooked my line and then swum off with my rod in tow; but shading my eyes from the sun, I saw that the splashing was caused by a swimmer, floundering wildly in the water. I was all set to row over when he suddenly struck out strongly for the shore. Still apprehensive for his safety, I watched his progress intently, breathing a sigh of relief when he reached land . . . but watching him struggle out of the water gave me the creeps. For one thing, though the distance was close to a half mile, I could see that he was fully clothed. For about thirty seconds he stood there on the bank, the water dripping from his sodden clothing. Then he lurched into the woods.

It wasn't walking in any sense of the word or motion. Lurching was the only thing I could find to describe the swaying, uneven gait of the man. I was appalled, yet unable to turn my gaze away from the grotesquely obese fellow. It was almost as if he had crawled up out of the slimed bottom of the lake and taken his first awkward steps on two feet. When I could no longer see him, the horrible fascination left me, but with a weak and nervous feeling in the pit of my stomach. I fervently prayed right then and there that I should never have the dubious privilege of meeting the fellow, under any circumstances. Anyone who went for a Sunday swim in his clothes and walked the way he had walked was not anyone I ever wanted to know.

Rowing back to my camp, it occurred to me that my vacation was rapidly turning into a full-scale

disaster. I could not remember when so many things had happened to disturb or infuriate me in such a short span of time; then again, my life had not been much more than an easy-going, peaceful chain of minor successes and achievements, hardly the breeding ground for any real mishaps or excitement — indeed, the one thing in my life I might point to with pride was that I had somehow survived a brief tour of duty as a medic in Germany, and I had found that to be more terrifying than exciting — but still, how much could happen to an inconspicuous, mundane fellow like me? I finally concluded that I was over-reacting to things in general because of the new scenery and the new people who came with it. I felt a lot better after that, and even found the courage to brew another pot of coffee while reading one of the books I had brought with me. I just had to take things in stride, I told myself. Besides, I could always get a good deal on another rod from Calvin.

*   *   *

I found the Langdon house to be a neat, two-storey affair nestled back from the main street in a grove of enormous oak trees and brightly "decorated" in front with beds of heart's-ease and begonias. Calvin answered the door when I knocked and quickly ushered me into the living room where I was introduced to Mary, his wife, and the Langdons — Sam, Rachel and their five-year old daughter, Becky.

Inside, the house was furnished in what most "city folk" try so diligently and fail so miserably in attaining; that is, the style and *atmosphere* of early Americana. Everywhere was the rich honey colour of polished wood and it was the Langdon family that made it shine. They radiated an aura of quiet, rustic contentment that enveloped you as soon as you stepped into their company. They greeted me with genuine warmth and without further delay we all went to the dining room and sat down to supper, Rachel and Mary serving the food and little Becky saying Grace in her childish, lisping voice.

The conversation never stopped as we ate our dinner. I found out that Sam Langdon owned a successful feed store in a town twenty miles away, catering to the needs of half the farmers in three counties. In a deep, booming voice that perfectly suited his strapping frame, he regaled us with stories about his store and customers until our sides were splitting with laughter and Rachel had to admonish him in her quiet voice that Sunday supper was not the evening funny papers. She was a younger, prettier version of her sister Mary, austere but gracious and friendly. I had no doubts about the happiness she shared with Sam and Becky. After dinner, she took her daughter upstairs for a bath and bedtime while the rest of us went back into the living room for tea and yet more talk.

"You sure ain't got no luck at all, Mr. Damon, do ya?" roared Calvin, after I had related my tale of "the one that got away . . . but with my fishing pole, too."

"No, I guess not, Calvin," I answered good-naturedly; "though in accepting your dinner invitation, it seems to be improving. I had no idea how much I was missing out there in the woods."

Calvin, Mary and Sam each assured me that I was welcome any time and then Mary went over to the piano and played a few songs, singing softly until Rachel came downstairs again with a worried frown on her face and hushed us all to silence.

"I thought I heard a wolf howling out in the woods just a minute ago," she said, turning a concerned glance back upstairs. "I hope it goes away. Becky is scared to death of noises like that during the night."

Suddenly, far off in the distance, all of us heard a mournful baying that was joined by one or two other wolves in a ragged chorus of howling that grew louder in volume with each passing moment . . . and then a shrill wail of terror echoed down to us from the second floor!

Rachel was the first one back up the stairs, but the rest of us followed her into Becky's bedroom to find the little girl huddled in her mother's arms and sobbing uncontrollably.

"There was a face, Mommy," she whimpered. "In the window and it was all white with big black eyes staring at . . . "

"Hush, Becky," soothed Rachel. "There wasn't anyone staring at you. It was just a bad dream, honey."

"No, Mommy, no!" cried the child, burying her face against her mother's breast. "It was all white with big black eyes and there was a hole in her neck and lots of greenish things crawling in and out."

Becky's vivid description of her nightmare settled an embarassed confusion over us all as we left Rachel to quiet her back into sleep. Needless to say, the little girl's fright put such a damper on any further light-hearted conversation that we sat about the living room in awkward silence. Rachel rejoined us a few minutes later, but it was plain that both she and Sam were anxious to be upstairs with their daughter.

"I guess we should be goin', anyhow," said Calvin judiciously, aware of their uneasiness. "T'morrow's a workin' day fer most of us and Mr. Damon here's gonna need all the sleep he can get so's t'be fit fer wrestlin' with them big ones on the lake."

Mary nodded her approval as Sam and Rachel smiled gratefully. Our "thank you's" were brief and soon after, the Adderleys and I were walking in the sultry heat of the evening, bathed in the wan light of a gibbous moon that had just risen over the treetops.

"Come round first thing in the mornin', Mr. Damon," said Calvin, passing an arm around his wife's waist to squeeze her affectionately. "I'll see what I can do 'bout sellin' my best rod at cost . . . t'replace the one that got away."

"What Calvin means is that he'll do just that, Mr. Damon," advised Mary with a mock-serious expression. "He's got the heart of an angel most of the time, but when it comes to business I do believe he's got the soul of a pirate. Don't you give him a penny more than sixty percent of the price tag, you hear?"

All three of us broke into soft laughter that carried us to the porch of the Adderley's house; but as I waved "Good night" and started back to my car, the stillness of the night was again broken by a muted chorus of howling that seemed to crawl through the heavy night air. I stopped dead in my tracks to listen to it, glanced behind me to see Calvin and Mary doing the same on the porch.

"Wait up a bit, Mr. Damon," he called quietly when it had faded into silence. "Be out in a second."

I heard him fumbling nervously with the keys to the front door and lit a cigarette, my first in days, while trying to puzzle out his reason for asking me to wait for him. As I smoked, I saw the lights flash on in the kitchen and Mary's silhouette against the curtains as she busied herself with one thing or another there. A moment later, the lights went on in the upper storey and before I had smoked half my cigarette, Calvin had reappeared on the front porch.

"What's going on, Calvin?" I asked, noticing the sober expression on his face.

"Nothing', Mr. Damon, nothin' at all," he replied quickly. "Ain't no harm in takin' precautions, that's all. You just take this along with ya and I'll be seein' ya in the mornin'. G'night now."

"Good night, Calvin," I murmured, staring down at the .45 automatic he had pressed into my hand.

THREE

It didn't take me long to realize that there was more to Calvin's offering me his pistol than met the eye. As I left the tree-girt lanes of Thatcher's Ferry behind, plunged out onto the moon-bright, dusty ribbon of road east of the town, the silvery light streaming through my windshield struck upon the blue steel of the pistol where it lay on the dashboard before me. It *seemed* as if Calvin had pressed it upon me as protection against the wolves, the immediate result of the baying we had heard twice thus far in the course of the evening . . . but my own small knowledge of such things told me that wolves, unless goaded by the killing hunger of a severe winter or some other catastrophe, were instinctively loth to venture anywhere near to Man or his haunts. Why then Calvin's unwarranted alarm at the mere sound of two or three wolves giving tongue . . . unless he had some further reason for arming me that he had chosen not to relate. His *extreme* agitation upon hearing the wolves gave credence to this possibility . . . but the pistol was no more than a mute witness to my inability to answer the question I had put to myself. When I turned off the road and onto the narrow track that wound through the woods to my campsite, I shrugged off my perplexity and directed all my attention to negotiating the difficult twists and turns that loomed in rapid succession before my jouncing headlights. Not wishing to risk a broken axle on such uneven ground, I slowed the car to a cautious crawl and so made my way back to the lake-shore.

I must own that I was not in a very relaxed state of mind when I reached the lake, in spite of my earlier resolve to take everything in stride. Unconsciously, the many events of the day had wrought heavily on my nerves and as I switched off the ignition and doused the headlights, an intense dissatisfaction settled over me that I could account for in no other way. Irritably, I slammed the door of my car shut and stood unmoving in the gloom, where no hint of moonlight might find its way down through the trees to irritate me further with its unwinking stare. I glared out over my campsite, half-silvered and half in shadow; at my boat on the shore and the glimmering, ghostly expanse of the lake. I felt as if I might never again see so bleak and empty a scene as this utter solitude. It was quiet, so very quiet that my ears strained to hear a sound in the stillness, ached with the violence of their questing. I realized that it was *too* quiet; that there should have been rustlings and croakings and crickets doing whatever it is that makes their cricket noises. There should have been at least a whisper of a breeze in the treetops . . . instead, there was nothing . . . and I was amazed at how quickly my unsettled state was changed to a distinct uneasiness that squirmed in the middle of my stomach. My hand leapt through the open car window and fastened itself around the cool, flat grip of the automatic

God knows why, I slipped the safety catch off immediately and took a timourous step forward, my neck prickling with tiny streams of perspiration. The dark canopy of trees overhead no longer seemed sheltering, yet with each step towards the half of my camp that was bathed in moonlight, I felt increasingly reluctant to leave the comforting solidity of my automobile behind me. Soon, my outstretched fingers slid off the front fender, casting me adrift in the narrow swath of blackness that yawned every which way. My eyes focused wildly on the unwavering line where darkness became light . . . and I smelled Death.

With every step it crowded close around me,

forcing its noisome odour into my nostrils and down into my lungs. In the absolute stillness, the stench seemed to lie stagnant; a tangible, clinging vapour through which I had to claw my way forward. It was the claustrophobic atmosphere of a charnel house — a bubbling melange of decayed flesh and mouldering cloth — conjoined with the rank swill of a coffin-less grave. I was suffocating in it. With a strangled cry that was smothered by the air even as it leapt from my throat, I ran into the chill light of the moon . . . towards the lake . . . felt my right leg slipping out from under me . . . sprawling flat on my back.

I felt a curious wetness seeping through the canvas of my shoe. Elbowing myself up, I saw the toe stained and glistening in the moonlight. I rolled on my side, coiling my legs beneath me, pushing myself up with my left hand only to have it, too, touch upon slick wetness and slide off in betrayal to my desire to run. On my stomach, inches away from my face as I struggled to rise, I saw that which had caused me to fall.

They had once been living creatures of the wood — perhaps raccoons or badgers, or both — but now they were nothing more than a heap of darkly-stained tatters of fur and raggedly torn limbs. Three of them, half a dozen . . . I couldn't tell . . . all joined in a hideous, pitiful mound of violent death. A small, bandit-masked face stared at me out of the centre of the carnage with glazed, pain-maddened eyes. A sickening lurch in my stomach told me that these hapless beasts had been torn apart while yet quick with life; and while I scrambled to my feet, unconsciously wiping my blood-soaked hand on a trouser leg, I heard a branch snapping behind me.

"Who's there?" I screamed, whirling about with .45 held high. The moon was at my back, flooding over my shoulder into the woods that curved off along the shore of the lake. All was quiet, deathly still, unmoving.

"Answer me, by God! or I'll shoot . . . wherever you are. . . ."

Silence of the grave. Shadows of questionable substance that lurked and skulked in noiseless mockery, beyond the reach of the moon's silvery fingers of light. Wordlessly, I prayed for something to present itself as a target to my pistol . . . something real, not just the empty dead stillness, the smell of those poor mangled creatures's agony strangling me by inches at a time . . .

I looked at my outstretched hands with their knuckles bone-white around the pistol grip and saw that they trembled violently. Empty threats, I muttered to myself, lowering them weakly. You couldn't hit an elephant at ten paces . . . and I laughed softly, hysterically, at the thought. Poor furry little beasts . . . so neatly hacked into your bloody circle of dissolution.

"Aren't you going to try and tear me apart, too?" I shouted into the night. "Move, damn you! I know you're out there!"

Something did move . . . or at least, my eyes thought they saw something move . . . a lump of amorphous shadow between two treetrunks . . . then another . . . and another. . . .

"Come and get me, too!" I cried gleefully. "Come and get me or I'll shoot!"

The shadows didn't answer. They churned away soundlessly, like ghosts.

"Last chance! If you don't answer me . . . now . . . I swear . . ."

But they didn't answer and suddenly my pistol was up again, spouting flashes of fire into the woods. I couldn't be sure. Was I firing at *real* shadows that crawled away into the darkness? Was it me, shrieking like a damned idiot all the while . . . ?

I kept firing until the clip was empty, yelling until my throat was raw. The shadowy things had stopped moving . . . gone away . . . if they had even been there at all. At least it wasn't so damned quiet anymore. A flock of geese had risen in squawking consternation over the lake. In a daze, I ran to my car and the ignominious comfort of terrified flight.

FOUR

I remember getting incredibly drunk one Friday evening, when work and various other facets of my life were not quite what I wished them to be. In fact, that is all I remember of that evening because I awoke the next morning and found myself comfortably (discounting my hangover) in my own bed, in my own apartment, with my car parked outside. I was rather violently amazed by the whole thing. While my poor stomach lurched and churned and heaved, I wondered just how I had managed to drive three miles of city street, neatly parallel-park my car between two others (something I had never done properly before) and stagger up to my bed . . . all the while in a state of blind, stinking intoxication. After wondering, I muttered incoherently for a few minutes, took two aspirins and went back to bed with the unshakeable certainty that a small miracle had occurred, an inexplicable instance of what could only be termed "divine intervention." Now it had happened a second time.

When the haze of delirious terror had lifted itself

from my senses, I found myself hurtling along the road back to Thatcher's Ferry. Somehow, I had blindly, instinctively re-negotiated the track through the woods without killing myself in the process. No longer frightened, I was even ashamed at having been so in the first place. Spooked by shadows, I sneered at myself, lighting a cigarette and slowing the car to a more reasonable rate of speed.

"You *should* go back," I said aloud, exhaling viciously through my teeth.

I was suddenly very angry at Corey Thatcher. It was he who had left the grisly heap of helpless animals in the middle of my camp. As far as I was concerned, he had wantonly murdered them in order to scare me away and the thought was infuriating. Still, I couldn't face those torn bodies again. I looked down at the dark streaks on my trouser leg, at the pistol beside me on the front seat, and shivered.

It was almost eleven when I drove into Thatcher's Ferry for the third time that day, vainly trying to figure out the most sensible way of asking Calvin and Mary if I might borrow their couch for the rest of the night without really having to explain why. I need not have bothered, for as I searched among the trees for the Adderley's driveway, I heard the roar of another car approaching the town from the opposite direction in which I had come. A moment later, a battered pickup truck careened wildly onto the street with its horn blaring and bore down upon me at a headlong pace. I swerved, narrowly avoiding the truck as it flashed by, heard the squeal of its brakes and the gritty hail of dirt and gravel sent flying by its tires. Then I was out of my car and stalking irately back to give the driver a piece of my mind.

"What the hell do you mean by . . . ?" I shouted over the drone of the horn, but I checked myself when the door on the driver's side opened.

A man literally fell from the cab to sprawl in the dust at my feet, and as porchlights from homes nearby began to criss-cross the street I saw that his clothes were little more than rags hanging about his mauled and very bloody person. He crawled, dragged himself forward, lifting up his head as I knelt beside him.

"Edith . . . the kids . . ." he groaned, collapsing in my arms. "My God, they got 'em all . . . "

The lower half of his face was every bit as ragged as his clothing and I shuddered, wondering how human speech could possibly find its way through such a welter of blood and mangled flesh.

"What are you talking about, man?" I cried. "What happened . . . ?"

"They came . . . out the woods . . . " he said dazedly. The travesty of muscles and flesh about his jaw moved as he spoke, the words bubbled out like someone trying to speak through water. " . . . Was lockin' up the cows . . . in the barn . . . Edith and the kids . . . on the porch . . . I heard screamin' . . . growlin' . . . ran out . . . God! they was all over . . . comin' fer me and I couldn't do nothin' . . . The truck and got away . . . chasin' after me . . . Edie and the kids they got 'em all . . . "

He screamed the last words — a horrible, choking scream that sent a froth of blood gushing from his ruined lips. His eyes rolled wildly and I realized that a crowd of townspeople, awakened by the horn and squeal of tires, had crept up around us.

"Who came?" I pressed him, motioning for someone to call for a doctor. "Who did this to you?"

"Wolfs," was his garbled reply. "Dozens o' wolfs . . . comin' this way . . . and they got Edie and the kids and I ran away . . . "

A horrified murmur ran through the crowd. The fellow began to sob, what was left of his face twisting into an agony of grief. I was grateful when a thin wisp of a man in trousers and a nightshirt elbowed me aside and opened his black bag. As I staggered out of the circle I came face to face with Calvin and Mary.

"What're you doin' back here, Mr. Damon . . . Good Lord! What you been up to, anyway?" He was staring at my now blood-soaked shirt and trousers.

I shook my head and waved a nerveless hand behind me. Calvin went on to investigate as Mary took my arm and guided me to the much-needed, upright support of a tree. My knees were beginning to feel a bit like rubber. Calvin was back in an instant, his face white as a sheet.

"Do you know him, Calvin?" I asked weakly.

"Just barely," he replied tonelessly. "Name's Carl Vandermeer. Owns a farm up the county line 'bout thirty miles or so. Doc chased us away but he looks real bad. Y'know what happened?"

I nodded. "I all but caught him when he fell out of his truck. He said that a pack of wolves attacked his house. Dozens. Coming this way. They got his wife and kids before . . . "

"Oh God, not again," whispered Mary, clenching a hand to her lips. She looked at Calvin and he looked at her and they both seemed to shrivel up in their skins.

"Again!" I exclaimed in surprise. "You mean this has happened before?"

Mary nodded dumbly in affirmation. "I . . . I think I'd best get back to the house and start lockin' the windows, Calvin. Don't stay out here too long . . . and bring Mr. Damon with you. He can stay indoors with us tonight."

Suddenly the rubber was gone from my legs.

"Wait a minute, Mary," I said; and then, turning to Calvin, "When was the last time?"

"Three years ago," replied Calvin soberly. "They come roarin' in and near ruined the whole town. We tried pickin' 'em off from upstairs winders but it waren't any good."

"Did you have any kind of warning then?" I demanded.

"Nothin', Mr. Damon. One minute it was all quiet and the next minute all Hell was breakin loose. Twenty-odd devils tearin' everythin' t'pieces. It was late so there waren't nobody outside t'get hurt but . . . "

"Why didn't you say anything about it yesterday?"

Calvin looked at me queerly before answering. "It ain't the sorta thing folks wanna talk about, Mr. Damon . . . or even remember if they can help it. Being' so helpless and all ain't . . . "

"Vandermeer said there were dozens, Calvin," I said pointedly. "If that's true, you can't possibly lock yourselves in and expect the best. From what I gather, they attacked his family without provocation and that means they're blood-hungry; that your house may not be proof against them this time around. We've got to meet them *outside* Thatcher's Ferry at all costs, where they can't trap us in any confined spaces."

"Mr. Damon, you don't know what it was like three years ago," he groaned. "There ain't nothin' we can do fer it."

"I don't care what it was like three years ago!" I cried, furious at his stubborn refusal to see sense. "The fact is that they're coming now, they've wrecked your town once and with a pack of this size, they can do it again twice over. We'll need rifles to head them off and handguns just in case they get in at close quarters."

He stood vacillating for a dozen, angry heartbeats before turning to his wife.

"I guess Mr. Damon's right, Mary," he said with a sigh. "You better rouse all the men y'can over the phone. Have 'em meet in front of the church on the double. We ain't got much time."

Mary nodded and scurried away while Calvin

and I began recruiting among the rapidly thinning crowd clustered around Vandermeer and the doctor. News of the wolves had spread quickly and it was no easy task convincing anyone that the best defense was a good offense.

Even so, it was only a matter of minutes before Calvin and I had bullied ourselves a force of a dozen, armed men and a quarter of an hour later when thirty of us were jouncing along the westward road in a half dozen automobiles and pickups. Sam Langdon, Will Daley, Calvin and another fellow from the village rode with me in my car as we spearheaded the short column of vehicles into the outlying fields that surrounded Thatcher's Ferry on three sides.

"Have we got any high ground to hold against them?" I shouted above the roar of engines behind us. Calvin nodded bleakly from where he sat beside me.

"We're comin up on a string o' three, low ridges that front the south edge o' the forest-land," he said, pointing off to our right. "What with the dry spell we been havin', the ground oughta be solid enough fer us t'drive out t'the nearest one."

Thankful for this small bit of luck, I spun the wheel recklessly, stamped my accelerator pedal to the floor and sped out in a direct line towards the swelling mound of earth that glimmered in the light of the moon. With perhaps thirty minutes gone since the alarm was raised, we reached the foot of the southernmost ridge and clambered up the sere, treeless slope to its crest. As we gathered together there, I noticed with some dismay that only half of our small band carried rifles — which meant that unless our first volleys proved withering, we would have to face the majority of the wolves at a distance that was much too close for comfort. Hurriedly, and without thinking, I began to shout directives . . . until I realized with a start that another ominous, absolute quiet had settled over the countryside; that I need do no more than speak naturally in order to make myself heard to the others.

"I think our best bet will be to spread out along the top of the ridge," I began, surprised at the steadiness of my voice and amazed that everyone had instinctively hushed their nervous whispering to listen to me. "Ten feet apart with all our rifles on the flanks. We may not even see them if they've turned aside somewhere north of us; but if we do, everyone with a rifle opens up on them the minute they come over the ridge in front of us, shotguns and pistols when they hit the bottom of the slope. If they bunch together, then our centre will move a quarter of the way down the slope to meet them while the flanks slant in to pick them off from either side. If they fan out or try to outflank us, then we'll just have to move with them . . . and I'm not going to say we don't need a miracle (Another one, I asked myself wrily) to pull this off. If you've got any prayers, start saying them now. Otherwise, good luck."

One by one the men of Thatcher's Ferry filed out along the crest of the ridge, and by the taut expressions on their faces as they passed by, I knew there was not a one of them a whit less nervous than I was. There were a few moments of muted conversation as those with rifles arranged themselves by their own standards of marksmanship; then we laid ourselves flat on the dry, rustling grass to wait for the wolves, our ears straining to catch the merest hint of a sound in the unnatural silence around us. The very air itself seemed thick and fraught with a dread expectancy.

The minutes dragged on interminably as I gazed out over the landscape. Above us, the gibbous moon rode high in the star-strewn sky, casting a lurid glow over the hilltops. The scene before me was frozen into a picture of crystalline clarity — stark, unwavering outlines and shadows that, by their very stillness, filled me with unease. I closed my eyes and drew slow, deep breaths to quiet the sudden pounding of my heart.

"A-aren't you the guy who's fishin' the Thatcher lake?" asked a tremulous voice to my right. I looked over at a boy no more than fifteen or sixteen years old and nodded slowly.

"No need to keep your finger curled around that trigger," I advised him, noticing how white his knuckles were against the shiny black steel of his shotgun. "They'll give us plenty of warning . . . and yes, I am fishing the Thatcher lake . . . or I was up until now. Actually, I like some variety in my vacations."

I did my best to grin carelessly and could not have done too badly at it because he managed to return it with a relieved sigh.

"Thanks a lot," he said. "I'm Terry Sitwell and I'm scared t'death."

"Pleased to meet you, Terry," I almost laughed. "I'm Paul Damon and I am also scared to death."

It was a little better after that. Some of the others had heard our exchange and short bursts of nervous laughter released much of the tension that waiting had wrought inside of us. A glance at my watch told me it was 11:45 a scant forty minutes since Carl Vandermeer had collapsed in my arms. . . .

At 12:05 we were still waiting, but an ominous rumbling had drawn our eyes to the west where a low bank of clouds had appeared on the horizon. I cursed inwardly as a blistering wind soughed across the open farmland, driving clouds before it in roiling masses that swirled sullenly and bulked one atop the other. Soon, very soon, with a preternatural swiftness, we lay under a livid canopy that rapidly spread over the entire night sky, obscuring the moon and glimmering stars to leave us in total darkness. Ten feet of yawning, empty blackness separated each of us from our nearest comrade. A fork of lightening flickered away in the west.

"Good Lord preserve us," groaned a disembodied voice close by. "They're comin'!" I can hear 'em fer sure!"

A moment later, we heard the forest a half mile away erupt into frenzied life as an infernal baying scattered the smaller creatures of the wood into shrill flight. Another flicker of lightning snaked across the sky, closer, followed almost immediately by a ponderous roll of thunder. Having gotten a pair of clips for his pistol from Calvin and a shotgun from Sam Langdon, my place was in the centre of our formation. In the brief moment of light, I had risen to my feet and seen two dozen pale faces staring out into the night, unnerved twice over by the thought of facing the wolves in storm and darkness.

"We're in for it now!" I shouted over the continuous howling that issued from the woods. "Do the best you can. They're minutes away!"

Spatterings of what should have been welcome rain began to fall upon us, burgeoning swiftly into a steady downpour that crackled as it hit the dry grass at my feet. Through it all came the horrible ululations of the wolf-pack, the shrieking of hundreds of birds rising up from the woods into the storm-wracked skies. Gusts of wind swept across the open grassland, driving torrential rain into our faces and plastering our clothing in heavy folds upon our bodies. The sky exploded. Thunder rolled unceasingly in deafening blasts and then a massive bolt of lightning shot across the whole sky, tearing the clouds into tatters, illuminating our hilltop for another instant . . . and the wolves that had crept unseen over the opposite ridge!

Thirty frantic cries of warning were drowned in the wind as fifteen rifles began spouting flame into the mirk that joined earth and sky into one seething cauldron of chaos. Lightning rippled through the riven clouds with so much frequency that our battleground was almost continually lit in a stroboscopic glow. In this unholy light, we saw and engaged our adversaries.

Carl Vandermeer had certainly not underestimated the number of wolves in the pack that swarmed down the slope into the "valley" beneath us. Caught in the flicker and play of lightning, they seemed to move in slow motion, one close-packed, coarse-furred wave of snarling, slavering destruction. As they reached the bottom of the slope, they scattered under our rifle fire, leaving pitiful few of their number behind them . . . and in desperation I screamed into the wind, waving the farmers of Thatcher's Ferry down to meet them lest they run up and through our ranks and so have naught but open ground between them and the village. Halfway down the hill I met my first wolf.

From a loping cluster of six or seven it scrambled up the rain-slick turf and launched itself at my throat, fangs bared and dripping, its amber eyes lit by incredible fires of fury. Its upward flight seemed to take an eternity and all of a sudden, I felt a warm flood of wetness spattering my face and hands. Without knowing that I had done so, I had discharged one barrel of my shotgun directly into the grey-furred throat of the beast. Mangled by the heavy shot, it lay still at my feet with its life blood darkening the grass beneath its outstretched muzzle. Moments later, my second barrel left two more bleeding on the slope and I plunged into the centre of the fray.

To this day, I can scarcely surmise how I survived through the minutes that followed when, realizing the impossibility of re-loading my weapon in the maelstrom of rushing wolves, I turned it about in my grasp and, clutching the slippery barrels in both hands, flailed wildly at anything that moved on four feet. For all I could clearly see in the blinding downpour, I should have thought myself alone in the fight were it not for the heart-wrenchingly human cries of pain that I heard through the maze of my own terror. Again and again I felt the heavy oakwood stock thud into writhing, lupine bodies, arc into snapping jaws to shatter bone and tear sinew. Only once did I consciously have contact with another human being, and I thank God it was Terry Sitwell whose life it was I spared from the ravening hunger of the wolves.

In the glare of the lightning, I saw him down on one knee, trying to re-load a pistol with furious haste and totally oblivious to the great, snarling devil that streaked towards his unprotected back. Abruptly, he straightened up and took immediate aim at another wolf a score of paces before him . . . and then I had

elbowed him aside even as I swung my shotgun like a clean-up hitter reaching for the left field fences. The stock took the wolf cleanly alongside its head, splintering from the barrels as I heard the brute's spine snap like a broken twig. Then I was knocked sprawling to the ground by the lifeless carcass as the momentum of its final leap carried it full into my face.

Stunned by the impact, I slowly crawled from beneath the dead-weight of ragged, rank-smelling fur, still clutching tightly to what remained of Sam Langdon's shotgun, but shaken out of the frenzy that had kept me alive thus far. I was facing back up the ridge that we had held minutes before and there, unaware of my presence though I lay but a few feet away, was the largest wolf I had ever seen — a true black-furred monster of a wolf that glared imperiously from one side of our battleground to the other as if surveying the progress of its "troops."

I stared at this freak of nature with a mixture of fear and admiration, unable to turn aside my gaze until I felt it being drawn inexorably to the luminous orbs through which the wolf seemed to flash the crimson fire of its primitive hatred. Spellbound, I watched them flare with an uncanny light of intelligence and it lifted its muzzle to the thundering heavens to voice some howling command to its legions. Then it turned, almost disdainfully I thought, and began to climb the ridge in long, effortless strides. And I followed without ever reasoning why I should do so.

I climbed after it, slipping in the sodden grass, stumbling over dark shapes that lay unmoving in my path. I saw the wolf disappear over the top of the ridge and climbed faster, using the shotgun barrels to lever myself up the slope. When I reached the top, I discerned the monstrous thing hurtling across the fields in the direction of Thatcher's Ferry!

Never looking back, I leapt madly down the southern slope of the ridge without giving thought to the possibility of taking a dangerous fall. As I reached the bottom and raced off in pursuit, the storm that still raged over the countryside effectually shut out all sounds of the battle I had left behind. I moved in a cataclysmic nightmare of Nature's fury that numbed me to all but the sudden, stern determination to meet and conquer the monster that I followed.

I did not doubt that the sable-furred wolf held complete sway over the rest of the pack. Instinctively, from the horrid gleam of intelligence I had seen in its eyes, I knew that it went to Thatcher's Ferry with some terrible purpose . . . a purpose that must be opposed . .

. and so I ran on, heedless of the strain upon my body, my eyes fixed blearily on the few winking lights that marked the existence of the town amid the storm and darkness.

By the time I reached the village, the storm had ebbed in its intensity as quickly as it had come, until the clouds had dispersed into mere wisps and shreds scattered across the sky. I stood in the mired and runnelled main street, gasping for breath in the moonlight as rainwater clattered down off the eaves of the stores and houses along its length. Here and there as I strode about, I met lone wolves that I chased off by brandishing my steel "cudgel" and shouting incoherent threats; but nowhere could I find the black wolf. Cursing angrily to myself, I plunged into the shadows between the houses, often slipping or stumbling and no doubt frightening anyone who might have heard me more than ever a wolf should have done. Vaguely, it occurred to me that I might be mistaken for a wolf by one of the terrified residents, and shot accordingly. After that, I went more quietly, stalking the midnight-coloured beast as it would have stalked me.

Minutes, hours could have passed without my cognizance of their passage. The entirety of my awareness funnelled down into one burning desire to exterminate the anomalous thing that Nature had guised in the form of a wolf. My search became systematized, methodical and in deadly earnest . . . and in the moment when exhaustion would have reached out to encompass its end, I spied a brief fluttering of shadows behind one house that could be naught else but my prey. Fatigue fell away from me as I skirted another dwelling to head off the beast. I think I must have grinned with a fierce exultation as I sped noiselessly over the soft ground, turned one corner of the next house . . . another corner . . . and came face to face with the black wolf!

All the world hung suspended and breathless as I met the glare of surprise in those crimson-flecked eyes. The rattle of water in the drainpipes faded away into silence, the drip-drip of rain from the overhanging trees, all ceased to patter in my ears. The wolf stood back from me, a huge splotch of inky colour with flanks that gleamed evilly in the tatters of moonlight that found their way to our odd trysting-place. A low growl of anger rumbled in its throat as a challenge, or perhaps, a demand that I step aside. Of all things absurd, I shook my head in negative answer and gripped the shotgun barrels in both hands. It took a sideways step to avoid me and I moved with it, barring its way even as I noticed that it held something in its jaws — a small, mud-stained burlap sack.

Again it moved and I with it, more angry sounds issuing from deep within its massive chest. Carefully, it lowered its burden down, crimson eyes now filled with a blazing hatred that I should so seek to thwart its designs. I felt myself quail in that awful regard and, fearful lest I fail in *my* purpose, I raised my weapon and leapt forward with a strangled cry of terror and defiance.

My downward stroke whistled through empty space as the hellish creature's unnatural strength and agility carried it beyond my reach. Snarling, it whirled upon me like an express train, knocking me off balance as its rippling hide engulfed me. Between the seconds when I felt myself toppling and the glancing impact of my head against some immoveable object, I dimly heard my name being called and a succession of loud reports that must have been gunshots. Then all consciousness was buried in a wave of irresistible blackness.

*   *   *

"He's comin' round now! Get some o' that whiskey down from the cupboard."

I opened my eyes to a dizzy whirl of figures that quickly coalesced into a pair of familiar faces as the whiskey churned down my throat and into my stomach. Calvin and Mary stood over me anxiously, their faces pinched and drawn with concern.

"How ya doin', Mr. Damon?" he grinned feebly, and when I made an effort to answer he said, "No need t'say anythin'. Just nod. You had yerself a close call, ya know. We all did fer that matter . . . Lord alone knows how, but we managed t'hold 'em off just like ya said we could. Musta left three quarters of 'em lyin' out there and scattered the rest. Most of us got chewed up and scratched up a mite nasty . . . and there's five of us, God rest 'em, ain't gonna do no more worryin' . . . but there warn't nothin' else too serious and so I guess we done all right fer ourselves after all."

"Hush now, Calvin," chided Mary, nudging him aside. "Can't you see Mr. Damon's all set t'faint away again with all your chatterin'? Let him be for a while."

"No. It's all right, Mary," I protested, raising a hand weakly. "Please . . . help me up. I want to know what happened . . . How I got here. The last I remember . . ."

"Was takin' a nasty fall from one o' them that got away from us on the ridge," finished Calvin. He helped me to a sitting position from where I lay on their living room sofa and I noticed that his left hand was bandaged rather heavily, his face and throat furrowed by deep scratches.

"Ain't nothin' t'what you looked like a little while ago, Mr. Damon," he said soberly. "I seen ya once or twice out there, swingin' them shotgun barrels fer all ya was worth. It's a wonder yer all in one piece with all the wolves ya had crawlin' all over ya. Then again, most of us was just plain lucky t'make it through tonight . . . "

Vandermeer's family and five others dead, I thought. Some luck.

" . . . Funny thing is, them wolves waren't half so mad as I woulda expected."

"What do you mean, Calvin?" I asked, confused by his statement.

"I mean that they was vicious enough t'begin with, Mr. Damon . . . that's when *we* had our worst luck . . . but after they was finished doin' their first bit o' viciousness, there waren't no rhyme or reason t'the way they was roamin' around snappin' at the breeze. I remember when them first wolves came at me and I could see all the fire o' you-know-where burnin' in their eyes. Next thing I know them eyes is all dull and stupid . . . "

Mary held another shot of whiskey to my lips as I pondered Calvin's observation.

"You relax a bit while I'm gettin the coffee ready," she said softly. "You can talk all you like then."

She went off to the kitchen with a meaningful look at Calvin, who promptly set about making me more comfortable in a dutiful silence. I exhaled a long breath and sank into the pile of cushions and pillows at my back. Curiously, I examined a torn and bloodied heap of clothing that lay in the foyer, suddenly realizing they were my own; that someone had stripped them off me and tended whatever wounds I had sustained in the night's "activities." As the whiskey's immediate warmth began to wear off, and was replaced by numerous aches and twinges of pain, the true extent of the mauling I had received came home to me. I was in the middle of telling myself how happy I was to be alive when Mary returned with three steaming mugs and a coffee pot.

"You'll stay with us tonight," she said kindly. "Calvin says there's still a lot of wolves loose and besides, you're not fit to walk across this room, much less drive out to that muddy puddle of a campsite."

"Thanks very much," I smiled, accepting my mug none too steadily. "I think I'll be quite happy to collapse right here . . . but after you've told me what happened."

"Ain't much t'tell, Mr. Damon," said Calvin after receiving an assenting nod from his wife. He sat down in an armchair across from me. "Seemed like we was out there fer years though it's just edgin' past 2:30 now. At any rate, we all took a pretty fair beatin' fer our troubles, but it was like I said — once ya held out fer the first little while, it waren't no trouble t'do 'em in. The main thing was that there was so doggone many of 'em. We just kept firin' and swingin' and layin' 'em down like at a carnival shootin' gallery . . . and when the storm let up, them that was still kickin' took off with their tails tucked 'tween their legs . . . which was when I got careless and let one of 'em take a bite out of my hand.

"But it was over then. We started countin' heads and that was when we realized that five of us were . . . and that you and Darby Sitwell's kid was missin'. When the rain stopped, we started pokin' through the bodies, prayin' like heck we wouldn't find neither of ya buried underneath. Half an hour later we sorta slogged back into town and I came in here all tuckered out and fit t'die that you'd been cashed in on account of us. Thank God, there you were on the couch with Mary and young Terry sittin' over ya."

At that point, Mary took up the conclusion of the story, explaining how she had gone to the Langdon house to be with her sister and how they had sat fearfully through the storm, listening to the echo of gunshots and the howling of wolves that had gotten past us and into Thatcher's Ferry; how the storm had finally abated and she had ventured out onto the Langdon's front porch upon hearing Terry Sitwell's cries for help.

"He told me how you had saved his life out on the ridge," she went on, "and how he had seen you chase off after one of the wolves. Terry followed you after he got clear of the fight and again, when he saw you duck around towards the back of the Hodgson house. He said he couldn't see too well, but enough to make out that you were hurt and that there was a wolf all ready to snap at you. He fired his pistol high for fear of hitting you by mistake . . . but it was enough to scare the wolf off. Then he managed to drag you over this way and together, we got what was left of your clothes off of you."

"Did Terry find anything close by to where he found me?" I asked eagerly, at the same time making a mental note to offer my thanks to the boy.

"He didn't say anything to me," replied Mary. "How about you, Calvin?"

Calvin shook his head. "Nope. Not a word, Mr. Damon. You lose somethin' out there?"

"No, I didn't lose anything, Calvin," I replied hesitantly, "but I thought that the wolf was carrying something in its mouth, a burlap sack that it put down just before it attacked me."

"But that's crazy, Mr. Damon," said Calvin. "Wolf don't go carryin' burlap sacks around fer the fun of it."

"I know that," I mused aloud, "and yet I can almost swear . . . "

"Never you mind, Mr. Damon," interrupted Mary. "We'll just get you comfortable for sleep now." She laughed rather hollowly, and then murmured to herself, "Lord knows it's been a trying time for all of us . . . but poor little Becky the worst. She didn't sleep a wink. I've never seen her so scared in all her short life."

"Nightmares and howlin' wolves'll do that t'kids, Mary," said Calvin tenderly. "She's a perky one. Be fine in the mornin', won't she, Mr. Damon?"

"Yes," I replied wearily, "I'm sure she will."

Calvin gave me a queer look and I tried to act as if I had meant what I had said.

"Don't tell me ya think Becky seen what she said she seen," he demanded suddenly. I noticed a catch in his voice and inwardly debated whether or not I should be entirely honest in answering him.

"I don't know, Calvin. Thatcher did warn me . . . "

"Thatcher warned ya against wolves!" he exploded. "Not a kid's midnight hobgoblins!"

"True enough, Calvin," I replied evenly; "but how did he know they would show up here? And he didn't warn me specifically about the wolves either. Maybe he is crazy . . . and to the point of trying to get back at the people of Thatcher's Ferry for laughing at him all these years. But why the wolves all of a sudden? You yourself said that they acted strangely. And what about the dynamite he bought from Will? I can't explain any of it, Calvin . . . and I can't explain why the wolf that attacked me here in town was carrying a burlap sack . . . but it was and I'm certain of it now. There's more to all of this than I can see plainly . . . "

The three of us sat staring at each other in an uncomfortable silence. Nervously, Mary stirred herself up and began clearing the coffee table. When she was gone, Calvin spoke again.

"Wolves just come and go," he said stubbornly. "And Corey Thatcher's just plain loony. He can't do us no harm and there ain't nothin' else t'talk about, Mr. Damon."

"I'm not afraid to admit that I'm not so sure of *that*, Calvin," I said, looking him hard in the eyes. "And I'm not too proud to admit that all of a sudden, for no real reason, I'm uneasy enough to listen to Thatcher's advice and take my vacation elsewhere. I think I would, too . . . except that I've got the nagging feeling inside my head that something is going on here that's not quite right, something very much out of the ordinary . . . and like it or not, I'm a part of it now."

FIVE

In the morning, at least two other people in Thatcher's Ferry found a reason to be afraid, and I began to speculate wildly in an attempt to make sense out of the odd circumstances that would present themselves during the course of the day. While the Adderleys and I (in clothes borrowed from Calvin) sat at a late breakfast, Terry Sitwell came by, offering to retrieve my car from its forgotten place below the ridge. Minutes later, a haggard Sam Langdon knocked loudly at the kitchen door with the news that Stan and Myra Bishop's two month old daughter, Elisabeth, had disappeared during the night; that Myra Bishop had walked into the room they had converted into a nursery, found the window open and the baby gone from her crib.

"The county sheriff will be here in a few minutes and everyone is meeting at the Bishop house to form search parties," he said with a haunted look in his eyes. "I just can't believe it. Becky *did* see someone last night, someone who waited until there was enough confusion to cover a kidnapping."

92

A quarter of an hour later, almost the entire
population of Thatcher's Ferry gathered outside the
Bishop home at the edge of the town — the women
milling about wide-eyed and incredulous, the men all
bearing some hurt as testimony to their struggle the
night before. Personally, I felt like a survivor from a
steam-roller attack, but no one seemed inclined to
excuse himself from involvement in this new calamity
because of the one just passed. Stanley Bishop, the
baby's father, stood calmly by as the sheriff detailed
out the armed volunteers to search different sectors of
the Thatcher's Ferry area. While Sam, Calvin, Will
and I stood around waiting for our assignment, Terry
Sitwell drove up in my car and eagerly sought me out
amid the throng.

"Mr. Damon, you're not goin' t'believe this," he
whispered breathlessly, "but I got curious when I got
out t'your car and walked up over the ridge t'see how
many wolves we killed last night . . . You gotta come
back with me and see for yourself."

"That's going to be difficult right now," I replied,
and then explained the reason for the whole town
being gathered in front of the Bishop house.

"Can we get the area around the ridge?" he asked
insistently, and Calvin, standing nearby, went off to

see if it could be arranged. He returned a moment later, nodding affirmatively and Terry's explanation was put off as the sheriff voiced last minute instructions.

" . . . Before we get started, there's just a few things I want you folks to know. First off, whatever happens here is going to have to be done by us because that storm last night all but washed Belleville from the map. Every local agency with any kind of manpower is going to be tied up there for days.

"As far as we're concerned, I want you to know that some footprints were found in the nursery but they were too muddy and smudged to be of any help to us. Although the kidnapper must have come through the nursery window, there are too many wolf-tracks beneath that window for us to determine which way the kidnapper might have gone afterwards. The rain didn't help there, either. To be safe, we're going to have to cover three hundred and sixty degrees around this town . . . although with that pack out here last night, it doesn't look good for a long escape on foot. Be on the watch for signs of any overland vehicles. We'll just have to do our best and meet back here around suppertime."

At the mention of the wolves, Myra Bishop started

screaming hysterically and had to be taken inside the
house by a half dozen women, including Mary Adderley. Shortly after 11:30 A.M. the crowd broke up and
Sam, Calvin, Will, Terry and I began our trek on foot,
angling out towards the ridge that had been our
battleground of the previous night. Try as I might, I
couldn't induce Terry to further explain the cause of
his excitement and so we strode out over the fields in a
tense expectancy that was tempered by the fierce heat
of the sun as it rose to its zenith in the sky.

Though it was drying rapidly, the ground was
still waterlogged by the rain and our pace was madden-
ingly slow and tiresome. When we finally did reach
the crest of the ridge and looked down over the shaggy
carcasses strewn about the valley below, each of us
turned to Terry with a puzzled inquiry on our lips.

"Count 'em," he said simply, "though I can tell ya
right off there's only twenty-three dead wolves down
there. I thought it was strange 'cause I'm pretty certain
I was good for seven or eight myself . . . so I went down
and looked around some . . . and oh, I found this, too. I
saw you drop it right after you clobbered that wolf for
me, Mr. Damon. Thanks a lot."

Terry pulled Calvin's .45 from his pocket and
handed it back to me. Then he started down the hillside,

beckoning for us to follow. His initial observation had aroused our interest and scarcely ten paces from the crest of the ridge, a nauseous stench assailed our nostrils, the odour of a charnel-house full with decay that seemed to fill the trough between the two southernmost ridges — an odour so much like the half-forgotten odour of my campsite the night before that I had to clamp my teeth together in order to keep from crying out. Soon, we reached the first corpse and Will Daley stood a moment to scratch his balding head in bewilderment.

"I coulda sworn we killed somethin' like three or four times the number o' wolves lyin' out here," he exclaimed, wrinkling his nose at the stench. "And these don't look like they been lyin' around long enough t'stink the way they're doin', either."

"That's what I thought, Mr. Daley," cried Terry, "and then I noticed all this white stuff lyin' all over the place and that the smell was strongest wherever there was a lot of it."

The four of us converged on the spot where Terry knelt over a concentration of the white, powdery substance in question. Upon closer inspection, the noxious odour seemed to emanate not so much from the actual powder — which was clotted together by moisture in some places and exceedingly fine-grained where it had already dried in the sun — as from the patch of turf surrounding it.

"Whatta ya think it is?" asked Calvin, sniffing gingerly at a pinch between his fingers.

"I'm wondering what happened to all the wolves we killed last night," I replied. "I think Terry's right about that . . . but who would be crazy enough to come out here in the middle of the night and cart off dozens of dead wolves?"

"Same sort who'd scatter this white stuff around," snorted Calvin, "and we all know who that would be."

"Crazy Corey Thatcher!" shouted Terry and Will in unison. I shook my head.

"There's no sense to that and I'd like to know *what* this powder is before making any surmises about *who* is responsible for it being here."

"That's easily done, Mr. Damon," offered Sam. "Down at my store, we usually make spot checks on the chemical content of shipments of feed and fertilizer. One of my fellows could do a fairly thorough analysis if we could get a sample to him."

Terry volunteered even as I bent to scoop a sample

into a handkerchief, and after receiving my car keys for the second time that morning, started back to Thatcher's Ferry at an ambitious trot.

"The kid's taken a shine t'ya, Mr. Damon," grinned Calvin.

"We'd better get about the first business at hand," I said quietly, and my three companions concurred.

After traversing the pair of ridges that lay between us and the woods, we started off in a westerly direction in order to skirt the edge and soon turned back to the northeast. It didn't take us long to realize that both Elisabeth and her abductor stood almost no chance of being found alive in our sector. Scarcely a mile from the southwest corner of the woods, we reached the first farm along our way, a low split-rail fence marking the pasturage of Horace Granby's sheep. Halfway across the field we met Granby, standing over the mangled remains of one of his flock with a heavy-gauge hunting rifle held despondently in his hands.

"Damned wolves!" he cried, almost in tears as we approached him. "They come up so fast and I'd left the whole flock out for the night. 'Fore I knows it they done tore up three quarters of 'em just like this one here. They didn't stop t'feed or nothin' . . . just a pack o' devils bent on killin'. All they done was jump on one, ripped up its throat and went on t'git another!"

It was the same at each of the five farms we came to that day. The four of us grew more and more uneasy with each bloodied animal we found. The fields were littered with them, almost as if the wolves, not content with merely murdering off human beings, had launched also a concerted attack on the sustenance of Thatcher's Ferry and its environs, intent on destroying the livelihoods of its people and reducing the work of lifetimes to shambles and ruin. Each tale grew more bizarre, the one told us by the farmer furthest from town relating how the wolves had actually battered down his barn doors to get at the mares and chickens inside when their assault on the main house had failed. Of Elisabeth Bishop and her abductor we found not a trace.

"I guess we know why they took so long t'get from Vandermeer's place t'us," observed Will Daley, mopping the perspiration from his face with an already drenched handkerchief. "D'ya think maybe 'Mad Corey' coulda done the kidnappin'?"

"Becky said she saw a woman's face at her window," offered Sam.

"Yeah," said Calvin, "and she also said the woman had a hole in her neck with worms crawlin' in and out the hole. Mighta seen one thing and imagined another."

"I guess we'll find out about Thatcher tonight," I said wearily. "The sheriff did send some people out to his house, you know."

"Well, someone's gotta have better luck than us," muttered Calvin as we started back to town. "I mean, how far could anyone go in one direction or twenty with all them wolves tearin' hell outta anythin' that breathed?"

"Maybe it's better if nobody finds nothin' at all," wheezed Will. "Whatever anyone finds ain't gonna be pretty and the Bishops is close t'breakin' as it is."

It was a callous thing to say at that point, as we trudged back through the now fly-infested fields; but still, I had to give Daley a lot of credit. Of the four of us, he was the least suited to tramping miles in the merciless blaze of the sun, yet he had been no less dogged or uncomplaining than we had been . . . in spite of his ponderous bulk. We excused him out of general exhaustion.

Whatever gloomy thoughts followed in the wake of Will's remark, they were not voiced or, perhaps, I just didn't hear them. Hot, sweaty and dead-tired, my numerous cuts and bruises itching fiercely with the sun, it was too much of an effort to do anything but walk and try not to think the worst of what had happened. My thoughts were occupied by Corey Thatcher, wondering, in the light of my two encounters with him, if he were really crazy enough to steal the Bishop child as payment for the verbal abuse he had suffered from the townspeople. I couldn't make up my mind. Twice I had seen him and each time he had shown a different side of his personality . . . though I could still see the twisted smile he had bestowed upon me by the lake; but if he had not kidnapped Elisabeth Bishop, then who had kidnapped her? And why? The Bishops could afford no great ransom for the return of their child. The total wealth of Thatcher's Ferry might be considered the prize . . . but there were too many questions that had no answers. Where had all the wolves that we had killed disappeared to? It was insane. The whole damned thing was as crazy as everyone thought Corey Thatcher to be. Dead wolves did not disappear into thin air, nor did they create diversions for kidnappings. How could there have been human footprints in the Bishop nursery and yet not a one to be found outside? Even the rain had left wolf-prints outside the window . . . I thought of Corey Thatcher astride a monstrous black wolf with Elisabeth Bishop tucked under one arm . . . and then shook myself irritably. Either I was very, very tired or Corey Thatcher and I deserved to be roommates.

It was almost six when we got back to the Bishop house and by the expressions we saw on every face, we knew that an afternoon of searching had not gotten us any closer to the whereabouts of the baby. A lone set of extremely large wolf-tracks had been followed to and then lost in the woods surrounding the Thatcher lake and I surmised it had been the black wolf . . . but that left the Bishops with one last hope . . . the return of the group that had gone to the Thatcher house. They came in a few minutes behind us, reporting that they had found Corey Thatcher at home; that after telling him the reason for their "visit", he had paled visibly, but had allowed them to search his house from top to bottom, even answering their questions and cooperating fully.

"He looked as if he was hidin' somethin' t'me," said Zeb Wheatley, one of the men who had gone up there. "I think he done it but he's taken her somewheres else so's we can't find her."

If not for the presence of the sheriff, that remark might well have touched off an old-fashioned lynching party on the spot; however, he didn't leave until things were quieted down, saying that he would be back in the morning with some police experts and that Corey Thatcher should be left alone if only for the possibility that, if he were responsible for the child's disappearance, he might yet lead us to where he had hidden her away. By that time, it was plain that most people thought the Bishops had best start getting used to the fact that Elisabeth was gone from their lives for good.

"You'll stay with us again, Mr. Damon," said Calvin emphatically as Mary, he and I walked back to their house. "Wolves might be back, like as not. Y'can leave in the mornin' if ya want to. Ain't much else ya can do and it sure ain't much of a vacation gettin' involved in other folks's troubles. Don't think what ya done waren't appreciated though. There was plenty who seen ya and knew that you was the one saved this town from a lot worse than what's already happened . . . and that ya did it without bein asked.

"Fer me and Mary, it's been a pleasure. I'm hopin' ya'll come back again when things ain't so topsy-tur-vey."

A loud blast of a horn called our attention to the arrival of Terry Sitwell. As we neared the Adderley house, he pulled my car up to the front porch and waited for us with an ill-concealed excitement.

"I heard ya didn't find anythin' this afternoon," he said, ruffling a hand through his shaggy hair. "I'm afraid what I found out ain't gonna be much more than a puzzle, either."

"You got the analysis at Sam's store?" I asked eagerly. The boy nodded and his face became thoughtful.

"The fella that did it made three separate tests," he replied. "After the first one he said it was definitely bone 'cause a lot of their fertilizer has got bone ground into it . . . but he wasn't satisfied at that, said he couldn't be sure but there was differences from most of the bone he'd seen in fertilizers; that it just might be bone from a man or a woman!"

"Human bone!" I exclaimed, at a complete loss to find an explanation for such unexpected news. Terry nodded again, somewhat apologetically when he saw my confusion, and after returning my car keys, trotted homeward with a friendly wave of his hand.

"How d'ya explain that, Mr. Damon?" asked Calvin as we mounted the steps of his front porch.

"I can't explain it, Calvin. It's just one more mystery added to a long list of mysteries," I murmured aloud. "But the rest of it is exactly like the story you told me — a child disappearing and wolves laying waste to the countryside."

"What'd ya say, Mr. Damon?"

I realized that I had not even been listening to Calvin's theory on dead wolves and tentatively-analysed powder, being lost in the recollection of the strange events that had occurred in the time of Captain Elias Thatcher.

"Calvin . . . and Mary," I said quietly, "if you don't mind, I think I'd like to stay here until this whole thing get straightened out. I don't know if there's anything else I can do to help . . . but I've never done a damn thing in my life that's been of any real value or worth and I want it to stop right here."

"You're more than welcome, Mr. Damon," said Mary slowly, a bit perplexed by my request. "It's been rather nice having you around."

"Thank you. Thanks very much," I smiled, "but I'd like to go pick up my stuff at the lake. I know it's getting late but if I might hold on to your pistol a while longer, Calvin, I'll be safe enough and it shouldn't take me very long anyway."

At first, Calvin insisted that he go along with me, but I pointed out that he ought to stay with his wife and that I wanted to puzzle out a few things by myself. Grudgingly, he went into the house to get me another clip for the .45 and then I drove off, saying that I would be back before Mary could have supper on the table and not to worry.

It was good advice to offer, but hardly a true reflection of my own feelings. I *was* worried. As I sped along the road to the turnoff into the woods, a dire sense of premonition settled over me; that something more terrible than wolves or the kidnapping of a child underlay the curious events of the past three days. Try as I might, I couldn't find any logical patterns or connections between them, but intuitively, I was sure that each abnormality had a cause and effect that bore upon the others. A key was missing, a key that would let fall the pieces of the puzzle into their proper places. I felt that Corey Thatcher's tirade, his warnings to me, Becky Langdon's "nightmare," the Bishop abduction, the wolves and the white powder that might be human bone were all part of one and the same thing. It disturbed me to think that there was a hidden purpose behind the rash of tumultuous upset that had suddenly overtaken the sleepy town of Thatcher's Ferry . . . and I found my thoughts, my suspicions, all coming to rest upon Corey Thatcher.

My camp was a mess, nothing but shreds of tarpaulin remaining of my tent and sleeping bag beneath the willow tree. Only bones remained of the pile of dismembered animals. My boat was ten feet from the shore, half submerged by water, the wolves that had gotten through our defences on the ridge obviously having gnawed through the painter and then sunk it with their weight. I found my dented tackle box in a clump of reeds, its contents scattered over the clearing. Teethmarks covered all my light-weight aluminum cooking utensils and my cooler had been battered open though none of my food had been touched. In fact, there was nothing salvageable in my camp except for the few lures I could find and a scaling knife whose handle had been reduced to splinters. Daylight was waning. With a shrug of resignation and a last farewell to what had begun as a pleasant vacation, I turned back to my car.

The wolf stood directly in front of me, its red-rimmed eyes glaring, cutting off my path to the car. It was a shaggy, grey giant of bristling fur, standing motionless with its tongue lolling wetly from its fanged jaws. A low rumble came from its throat as I took a surprised step backwards, slowly drawing Calvin's .45 from the waistband of my trousers. Keeping my eyes fixed on those of the beast, I fumbled for the safety catch. The wolf growled, took a step forward . . . and sprang even as I whipped the pistol up and fired!

I don't know whether or not my shot found its mark for in the next instant, I was buried beneath the snarling fury of the wolf's attack, the automatic jarred from my hand as I fell heavily to the ground. I gasped for air through its dense, matted fur, my left hand raised to fend off the snapping jaws that sought to reach my throat, my right hand scrabbling madly for the chewed handle of my scaling knife. The beast's hot, stinking breath swirled into my lungs, sickening me to the verge of nausea and still I thrashed wildly in terror. My hand grasped the knife even as I looked again into the unholy amber glare of its eyes. Its weight on my chest was unbearable. I couldn't breathe. Sobbing, my heart beating my blood like hammer strokes on an anvil, I struck desperately with the knife, over and over again, tearing ragged holes in the squirming body above me.

I was all but unconscious when the wolf finally went limp, the unnatural light in its staring eyes dimming and then going out altogether. Painfully, I dragged myself out from under the carcass, drenched with its blood and bleeding from a score of newly-opened scratches and gouges in my own flesh. My brain screamed for me to get to the car before it was too late. One wolf meant others and as I staggered to my feet, I saw that it was so. There were three more wolves come between me and escape . . . and one of them was the black wolf!

A series of short barks came from its mouth and with an uncanny precision they separated, making sure that I could not reach my car without first encountering one of them. Slowly, they backed me towards the lake, growling loudly to summon the rest of the pack to aid in bringing me down. One of the grey wolves sniffed at the still-warm body of its brother and then raised its muzzle to glare at me with an almost human look of anger kindling further the yellow glow in its eyes. I turned, and found another group of beasts advancing towards me along the shore of the lake. Then I ran.

My flight became one long, torturous nightmare of unbridled fear. I ran, stumbled and crawled through the dense woodland, conscious only of the snuffling horrors that padded close behind me. The twilight of evening deepened into night as I ran on, heedless of the branches that stung at my face or the briars that tore and clung to my clothing. Each moment I expected to be pulled down from behind and ripped apart like the cattle I had seen that afternoon. My breath came shorter until it rasped in my lungs and a sharp ache began to pull at my side . . . and still I had to run because the wolves were relentless at my heels. I realized that they were toying with me, prolonging the agony of dread and suspense by keeping just close enough for me to hear them. It was four miles by car to Thatcher's Ferry. I didn't delude myself by thinking I could outrun the wolves even half that distance . . . but I didn't want to die. I kept my feet at all costs, knowing that the moment I went down, they would be on me and it would be all over.

Soon I was struggling uphill and then out onto a moonlit track that was clear of trees or brush and rutted deeply with tire treadmarks. I hazarded a backward glance and saw at least a dozen of my pursuers emerge from the woods and lope casually after me, led by the satanic shadow that was the black wolf. Their fanged mouths seemed to grin in the moonlight as they quickened their pace to a trot, anticipating an end to the chase. I was numb with fear and exhaustion as I rounded a bend in the lane, but the outline that loomed before me suddenly brought a cry of relief from my throbbing lungs and spurred me to one last burst of speed. It was a house! And the door was not a hundred yards away!

Grimly, I clenched my teeth and by sheer dint of will forced my body to respond. The wolves began to howl, surprised at my sudden sprint. The door was seventy-five yards away and then fifty, but I heard them closing in on me. Twenty-five yards. Fifteen and

I gripped the splintered handle of my knife. Ten . . .
five . . . and I reached the porch, falling to my knees
beneath the first attacker. I struggled upwards, slashing
with the knife, only to be knocked down again as a half
dozen more leapt upon me. My left arm exploded
with pain, and the snapping jaws around me, the
gleaming red-rimmed eyes and the growls all faded
into insignificance as I wheeled to stare into the snarling face of the wolf that had *dared* to bite me. My knife
flashed in the moonlight. With all the strength I had
left in my body, I plunged it down into the beast's
skull, down through the fur and the bone . . . into its
brain. With it still clinging tenaciously to my arm, I
dragged myself to the door of the house, turned the
handle and stumbled inside. I must have been near
delirium, for as I wheeled to slam the door shut behind
me, I thought for an instant to see a tall, broad-
shouldered form standing above the black wolf that
howled in the lane . . . a man whose whiskered face was
twisted in a snarl of rage.

SIX

I lay on the floor for the longest time, my breathing slowly becoming less laboured while I contemplated the grisly thing yet fastened about my arm. I was safe! The thought was uppermost in my mind, unable to be dimmed by the frustrated howls of the pack outside the door or even by the dull ache that had begun to creep through my left arm. Gingerly, I rolled on my side and extricated my arm from the rictus of the wolf's death snarl. The moonlight coming through the narrow glass panels on either side of the door glinted on the steel pommel of my knife, atop the small pillar of splintered wood that stood imbedded in the beast's skull. I knew it didn't matter, but I couldn't bring myself to pull it out. I sat upright with my back against the door and wept, draining the tension from my overwrought body and nerves. Then I remembered that the house belonged to someone I had not yet even seen. It was dark, but the moonlight reached far enough into the house to illuminate the newel post of a balustrade . . . and the checkered flannel shirt hanging there that belonged to Corey Thatcher!

It occurred to me that it was Thatcher I had seen outside when I slammed the door behind me and I leapt to a glass panel and peered through it . . . but if I had seen him at all, he was gone now. There were only wolves on the other side of the door.

I almost laughed out loud. To have escaped from the wolves to find myself at the mercy of a madman, a kidnapper and only God knew what else . . . and in his house, that was the crowning irony. It was very amusing to me at the time, but only long enough for me to realize that I was effectually imprisoned there for the night.

After summoning up my courage, I finally found a bathroom in the darkness of one of the lower corridors of the house, bathing the punctures in my arm and the numerous scratches added and re-opened on the upper part of my body. Thankfully, I saw that the puncture wounds had not bled too profusely, allaying my fear that a large vein might have been cut by the wolf's jaws. It would be painful for a while . . . but it was nothing serious. After binding the arm as best I could with a towel torn for the purpose, I went back into the main hallway and noticed a glow from under a door at its furthest end. Slowly, I made my way towards it, leaning cautiously against the wall.

The room was obviously Thatcher's library and it, as I had assumed the rest of the house to be, was empty of human occupancy. The glow I had seen in the hallway was the soft light shed by an oil lamp that rested on a massive oaken desk in one corner of the room. Though I was exhausted, my curiosity again got the better of me and I helped myself to a stiff Scotch and soda while I took a tour of the shelves.

Insane or not, I found that Corwin Thatcher had a library that was enviable by anyone's standards. His shelves were filled with beautifully bound volumes by every major writer from earliest Greece to the present, so many that my head spun when I tried to keep track of them. There were tiny slips of paper in almost every volume, filled with scribblings that I assumed to be Thatcher's own, and my confusion with regard to him only grew worse.

It was in a tall case directly behind the desk that I came across names and titles that were totally unfamiliar to me; and then I realized with a shock that the entire case was devoted to volumes and treatises on witchcraft and magic! Corey Thatcher immediately became a warlock in addition to all the other titles I had previously bestowed upon him. At that point, however, the Scotch and my exertions had made me sleepy enough to scan the room for a comfortable-looking chair. I was far from happy at the prospect of Thatcher finding me asleep in his house, but I had no choice. A glance out the rear windows had shown me that a great circle of wolves surrounded the house and the ferocity of their howling was not in the least reassuring. Nevertheless, I had chosen my place for the night when I saw the ragged volume that lay open on the desk, its title page illuminated by the lamp beside it:

RECORDE OF ELIAS THATCHER
MASTER OF YE BRIGANTYNE, DESIREE,
1770-1776

All of my sleepiness vanished upon reading those carefully printed words that leapt off the yellow paper. A diary belonging to Elias Thatcher! Unable to contain my excitement, I settled into the chair at the desk immediately. In the volume were many strips of paper, but these were empty of Corey Thatcher's handwriting. Using them as a guide, and beginning with the first, I started reading the entries made in the spidery scrawl of Captain Elias Thatcher.

14 Maye 1775 This day cawte and sanke ye Turke in ye Tigris-Eufrates mowthe after takynge on her riche cargoe in whyche was includit twentie females bownde for ye Sultain's hareem in Ishtamboul. One wenche hath laide holde of my fancie. Mayhap I shalt tease with her this nighte.

"So Elias Thatcher was a privateer," I thought out loud, "and that would explain the gold pieces that Calvin and Will mentioned."

15 Maye 1775 Kerinna hath set fyre to mie bloode. Tis a madness in her. At her requeste I have put ye reste of ye women to deathe. Her eyes arte blacke as nighte and she hath wrenchit mie verye Soule with her bodie.

16 Maye 1775 As master of mie shippe, I wed us twain this verye day. She speaketh of Life everlastynge in ye serviss of her oune trew Godde. Also of a place where lieth greate wealth for ye takynge and wherebye this Spiritt maye bee fownde in its earthlie form. She doth propose a journie to this place.

23 Maye 1775 This daye went we a score of miles on ye sweeps up into Tigris-Eufrates mowthe. Kerinna sayeth an equal journeyinge on ye morrow shalt brynge us to owre landmarke.

24 Maye 1775 Made we owre beddes upon ye sandes. Shalt write no more untill we reache ye place of wat Kerinna calleth ye Antient One.

28 Maye 1775 Seven of owre foure score and twelve deade of ye sun fever. Kerinna hath bidden ye men to unearthe ye doore unto ye caverne neath a greate mownde of stone.

29 May 1775 Ye caverne is hie to ye lengthe of fiftie men, pillars raiseth to ye vaulte of ye ceilynge. Muche is broken in pieces. Ye form of ye Antient One in greate fragmentes. Kerinna hath spoken falselie of treasures. Ye men are muche unhappie with this, yet she bendeth them to builde sleddes to carrye ye idol to ye shippe.

2 June 1775 Alle is readie. We leaveth this place with alle haste. Three men hath been loste, I knowe not wherebie.

10 June 1775 Returne to ye shippe is of muche difficultie. Foure perisheth with ye sun's heate and two others. Ye image is safelie in ye holde. We travell downe again to ye open sea!

There were no other markers for the next fifty or sixty entries, but scanning them, I found they contained an account of the Desiree's voyage around the Cape of Good Hope, a stop on the Gold Coast in Africa to retrieve loot previously taken, and many explicit

references to the amourous inclines with which the
Captain and his mysterious young wife amused themselves during the long crossing of the Atlantic. Fever-
ishly, I turned to Corey Thatcher's next marker.

9 Novembre 1775 Heavie stormes delaye owre returne
yet muche strangeness hath come to passe. Whilst
abedde, I wakit thro ye nighte to finde Kerinna
wast not beside me. Twas dawnynge wen she didst
returne. . . . This daye wast fownde ye corse of
Hawkins, his throate torne and alle besmirkit with
bloode. Ye crewe wast most uneasie. They mutter
of beastes ashippe but Kerinna hath gone amonst
them makynge fearfull glances with her eyes. She
hath ye soule of a devill in her, fore ye men art
muche quietened.

10 Novembre 1775 Kerinna hath made spells to driveth
offe ye stormes! Naismith wast fownde deade in
like manner to Hawkins. Ye crewe doth her biddynge with ne'er a worde. I can denye her nothynge.

13 Novembre 1775 We reache ye harboure in Newe
Yorke towne. Kerinna wilt not abide ye disbandynge
of ye crewe but fore mie officers, sayinge they shalt
bee needful in ye transportynge of ye Antient One.
She goeth to finde a restynge place fore Him.

Again, there was a skipping of entries. I paused
for a moment, intrigued and not a little bewildered by

this tale that no one had ever known to exist; except, of course, for Corey Thatcher. I had no reason to doubt its authenticity, theorizing that Kerinna herself had, in all probability, saved the book from the flaming death that had claimed her husband's life on the night their home had burned to the ground; however, the ghastly deaths that had overtaken the Captain's sailors, and the mention of the stone idol, fanned my curiosity further and I was anxious to see if Kerinna had made any entries in the diary that might illuminate either of these things. I read on.

20 Novembre 1775 Kerinna hath returnit with goode tidynges. His image hath been crated in its fragmentes. We leaveth fore ye place that Kerinna hath fownde on ye morrow.

29 Novembre 1775 Trippe hath been made with muche successe. Ye Antient One nowe safelie in ye caverne and rebuildit with Kerinna's artes to its fulle heighte. Ye crewe sheweth much feare again, livynge in ye caverne unbeknownst to ye crofters. Hath made muche progresse in ye buyinge of farmes. Kerinna maketh a greate shew fore those who arte loth and maketh muche of her persuasiones bie lookynge intentlie with her eyes and so they cometh to owre termes soone after.

7 Decembre 1775 Kerinna hath made a conjurynge and ye men arte thrallt and witlesse. To raiseth ye Energie and ye Spirit of ye Antient One, He who is not to bee named, there muste bee ye bloode of ye livynge. Upon ye altar of stones from ye mownde in Persia, we firste did maketh cuttes upon ye bodies of ye men, therebie deliverynge to owreselfes ye heartes, ye eyes, and ye male partes of eache. Ye bloode wast cawte up in bowles of beaten golde and powred o'er ye said partes of ye men whilst Kerinna sayeth ye wordes of Power. Thus hath she raisit up three scores and sixteene in ye shape and lyknesse of beastes that shalt do owre biddynge.

8 Decembre 1775 I groweth wise in her ways and ye knowynge of her magicks. With alle thynges writ of yester daye, we didst ope eache of us owre veines and lett flowe ye bloode of owre bodies o'er alle, speakynge again Wordes to brynge ye Energie of ye Antient One to owre place of conjurynge and fille ye image with ye vigoures of His life. We leaveth ye caverne when owre worke hath been donne, to waite for ye morrow.

9 December 1775 Ye conjurie hath failit! Kerinna hath saide ye offerynges wast not of ye necessarie puretie. We must fynde a Soule unspoilt, mayhaps a beaste.

14 Aprill 1776 Kerinna hath loosit ye wolfs and gone with them fore a woman of ye village. She didst returne with a corse bloodied abowte ye throate, her owne mowthe besmirkt.

17 June 1776 Alle owre effortes hath come to nawte bee owre subjecte Beaste or Man. After muche ponderynge on bookes whyche we hath procurit, Kerinna hath fownde ye tyme to bee beste fore siche thynges as we proposeth on ye nighte of Midsummer Even. One subjecte more muste we fynde, a chylde of ye village.

22 June 1776 Again we hath failit. Alle wast donne accordynge to owre knowynge with a man-chylde of ye village. We arte not possessit of ye righte wordes, I thynke. Kerinna hath gone to fynde ye booke of ye Arabyan, Alhazredd, wherein tis saide ye magicks of ye loste landes arte helde.

7 Auguste 1776 Kerinna returnes withowte ye booke yet hath made in her minde ye impresse of ye wordes needfull. Tis not a man-chylde fore ye rite, but a girl-chylde livynge insteade. Kerinna speaketh allso of strife betwixt owre lande and ye soldierie of owre Englishe kynge.

11 Auguste 1776 We muste waite. Ye village hath been rowsed bie owre conjurynges. We arte sus-peckit of sorcerie. Todaye Kerinna hath come home with greate anger, afrontit bie a woman of ye village. We shallt build us a howse owte from ye towne fore owre privacie. There is warre with ye Kynge's men, butt I doe not thynke we shallt see awte of itt.

13 Auguste 1776 Kerinna doth yet holde mallice against them of ye village. Tho we mayst not again trie to raise up ye Antient One fore feare of discoverie, she doth intend to plague ye village-folke with ye beastes made bie her sorcerie. We shalt waite. Ye caverne hath grown safelie hid.

I sat back, aghast at what I had read thus far. Here was the key that brought everything together . . . but could I believe the words of Elias Thatcher? Had he and his wife really been versed in the arts of black magic? What of Corey Thatcher and his books? Was he too a sorcerer? Common sense said "No" . . . and all the wealth of our modern science argued against even the possibility of magic being a real and working force . . . but what else could explain the odd, unnatural onslaught of the wolves that yet howled outside the library windows? Nothing but a magical summoning, I answered myself. The Captain's account coincided exactly with the time element in Calvin Adderley's story. Now it was happening all over again with Corey Thatcher carrying on where his forebears had left off; with Corey Thatcher summoning up the storm on the ridge, calling the wolves down upon the town that his ancestour had founded. The diary spoke of sailors that had been turned into beasts and there flashed in

my mind a picture of Corey Thatcher as the great black wolf leading the pack. Were such transformations truly possible? I scanned page after page in a frenzy until I came to an entry written in a bold script that covered an entire page. The writing was not that of Elias Thatcher.

> *28 Februarie 1789* THEY HAVE MURTHERED HIM! THEY DIDST COME IN YE NIGHTE AND FYRED YE HOWSE! ELIAS HATH BURNT TO HIS DEATHE. BIE YE NAME OF HE WHO SHALLT NOT BEE NAMED, I SWEARE I SHALLT REPAYE THEM FORE THIS NIGHTE BEE YE YEARES LONGE AND DARKE IN WAITYNGE!

It was the writing of Kerinna Thatcher! Decades passed in her long life with only small notations that expressed an undying hatred for the murderers of her husband; brief entries that told of her ghoulish revenge upon any and all who chanced to wander into her clutches; how she used the blood of living beings to re-vitalize her body. Finally, her entries ceased with one laboriously written page:

> *3 Maye 1866* It has been too long. This bodye is worn from the magicks. Soon I muste die. But I shall

send forth my spirit to find another bodye and
return for my vengeance. The Antient One shall
yet walk upon the earth!

Blank pages followed after it, but one of Corey
Thatcher's markers yet remained and I turned to what
was, thankfully, the last entry in that book of horrors.

4 January 1902 At last, I am returned to the house of
my children. The body of Sarah Patterson serves
me well and I have not forgotten. The devil take
Tobias, I warned him against siring a son by that
half-wit girl. Amory is mad. The village has nothing
but trouble from him. I cannot risk trying to raise
Him . . . but I must make spells to ensure my being
lest Amory bring doom upon me with his madness.
Someday . . . someday I shall have my chance . . .
and the wolves again shall be my messengers of
Death to the world and the Ancient One will trample
the earth into dust and blood!

The light of dawn was just beginning to colour
the panes of the library windows when I closed the
book and sank back in a cold sweat of fear that no
amount of common sense or logic could dispel. I
realized with a shudder of disgust that the diary had
cast a spell of its own over my senses; that I, whilst
reading it, had actually begun to believe what I had
read. This was the source of my fear. If I, a reasonably

sane human being, had fallen to the malignant influence of the book, then someone as unbalanced as Corey Thatcher must have done so irrevocably. He was behind it all, crazy enough to think that if his ancestors had tried to bring a stone idol to life, then he might also try. He had his own twisted reasons for wishing destruction upon the people of Thatcher's Ferry. All he needed, all he thought he needed was . . . a girl-child . . . on Midsummer's Eve . . . June 21st . . . Tonight! A girl-child tonight! He had stolen Elisabeth Bishop to sacrifice her tonight!

The sound of a car engine at the front of the house roused me to my own predicament. Footsteps sounded on the front porch. The front door opened, slammed shut.

"Empty!" came a muffled shout that whispered in the hallway. "They're empty!"

A moment later, the door of the library burst open and Corey Thatcher lurched heavily into the room. His clothes were smudged and dirty, torn to ribbons on his body. He was bleeding from a long furrow in his left shoulder. He stumbled in the doorway and I saw his eyes were fixed and unseeing. He fell backwards against the jamb and the dazed look left his eyes. I stood up slowly . . . and he recognised me.

"What are you doing here?" he growled, straightening and taking a step towards me. "I thought I told you to leave Thatcher's Ferry?"

"I . . . I *was* leaving," I lied, "but I was chased by wolves and found your house . . . by accident."

"I could kill you right now . . . here!" Thatcher menaced, raising a fist threateningly. "I could shoot you for trespassing, at the very least."

"You wouldn't be fool enough to do that, Thatcher," I bluffed in desperation. "You're in enough trouble already."

I cowed him with that. He lowered his fist angrily and stared at me.

"The little girl?" he said, shaking his head. "It wasn't my doing."

"The people in the village seem to think that it was, Mr. Thatcher," I replied hoarsely.

"I don't give a damn what they think!" he cried. "They searched this house. She's not here. If they weren't so stupid . . . "

"What about the cave, Mr. Thatcher?" I interrupted him. "What about the cave of the Ancient One?"

His head snapped upright, his eyes glaring as he looked at the book on his desk.

"So you've made yourself at home, Damon," he

accused dangerously; "taken it upon yourself to violate my privacy."

"I had nothing else to do," I stammered, then caught the rising note of panic in my voice with a challenge. "What about the cave, Thatcher?"

His face softened, then twisted into the cruel smile that I remembered only too well.

"You believe it all, don't you?" he sneered. "Or you don't believe it but you think I'm crazy enough to. . . don't you? You're just as stupid as the rest of them."

I didn't answer him and he grew agitated, pacing across the floor to tower over me.

"The cave doesn't exist, Damon!" he shouted in my face. "And if it does, I wouldn't know where to go looking for it. My ancestors were crazy enough to go in for that . . . but I'm not!"

"You knew I was here, Thatcher!" I shouted back at him. "Why are you acting out this farce? I don't know how you managed it, but I saw you herding those wolves after me. Why don't you just forget making excuses and denials and murder me the way you intend to murder Elisabeth Bishop?"

Somehow, I managed to meet and hold the baleful stare he leveled down at me. I thought for certain that he would hit me, but he clenched his hands tightly to his sides.

"Get out of my house, Mr. Damon."

"What . . . ?" I exclaimed, flustered and surprised. "I can't go out there. The wolves . . . "

"They won't bother you," he grinned sarcastically. "You've had your chance to make me into anything you damn well please! It's over. No more questions. Get out of my house!"

He stepped aside with a visible effort to control the wrath I had aroused in him; and I, sensing his restraint, contemplated one last show of defiance. I would show him what I had done to one of his precious wolves. He had obviously not seen it when he had come in, hidden as it was by the front door. My courage restored, I strode purposefully into the hallway, ignoring Thatcher though he trod almost on my heels . . . and then I stifled a cry of amazement as all my healthy, sane skepticism and logic fell apart, crumbled into chilly pricklings along my spine. There by the door, where I had left the carcass of a wolf with my scaling knife in its brain, was a brief scattering of white dust!

SEVEN

I stood as one turned to stone, staring incredulously at all that remained of what had been a wolf but six or seven hours before. The stench in the confined space of the hallway was overpowering, the same curious stench of my campsite and the ridge outside of Thatcher's Ferry. It was almost beyond my capacity to endure this time, but Thatcher was behind me and nothing else but pride kept my knees from giving out under me.

"Get out of here, Damon," he growled softly. I turned stiffly towards him, to see his reaction to the dust on his floor, but his face was totally impassive. "Get out of this town today or I can promise you will be very sorry."

He lifted his eyes to meet mine and nodded towards the door, imperiously, as if he knew that I would do nothing but obey him. Angrily, yet scarcely daring to breathe the nauseous fumes of the hall, I opened the door and edged slowly out into the watery dawn light that suffused the porch. Thatcher followed close behind.

"You see, Mr. Damon," he said with a hint of mockery in his voice, "it is just as I have said. The wolves will not trouble you."

The small open space surrounding the house, the rutted twisting lane that led away from it, were empty. Somewhere in the woods, a sparrow warbled cheerfully . . . and the wolves were gone.

"Damn you, Thatcher!" I said, but with no conviction in my words, "I'll stop you yet."

I heard him chuckling with a perverse amusement as he answered me. "I think not, Mr. Damon, though I do admire your tenacity . . . but I fear this affair is somewhat beyond your capabilities. I hope you will leave now, while you may yet do so freely and in a semblance of health."

I dared not look back at him as I strode down the lane. The wolves *were* gone, but for how long? I kept thinking that Thatcher could, in effect, murder me by recalling the wolves. It was not a heartening thought. Time and time again I forced myself *not* to look back or hasten my stride. Then I reached the point in the lane where I had emerged from the woods the night before and the urgency of my immediate return to town led me back along the path of my flight, back to the lake and my car.

I was amazed to reach my campsite in fifteen

minutes. The distance to Thatcher's house had seemed so much greater with the wolves chasing me. Vainly, I spent a few minutes searching for Calvin's pistol and then headed back to Thatcher's Ferry, the things I had read during the night and my third confrontation with Corey Thatcher reeling in my head.

I was not surprised to find that the wolves had invaded the town during the night. The fact that I now understood the mystery of those that had "disappeared" on the ridge — however far-fetched it might seem, I *did* believe that most of them had been sailors almost two centuries before, transformed by some sorcerous spell of "Witch" Thatcher's conjuring — made the carnage doubly frightening. Windows were shattered, doors scratched and splintered. The town seemed deserted as I came to a skidding halt in the middle of the main street. It wasn't until I had switched off the engine of the car that I heard the angry babble of voices from the far end of town and saw the mass of townspeople gathered around the low, wrought-iron fence of the cemetery. As I ran closer, I picked out Sam Langdon's tall form in the crowd and Will Daley's round, red face flushed crimson with emotion.

"Sam!" I shouted. "Where's Calvin? Is he all right?"

Langdon's head jerked around at the sound of my

voice and his eyes widened in disbelief as he saw me running towards him.

"Mr. Damon!" he cried, "We thought for sure that the wolves had gotten you last night."

"They almost did," I said breathlessly. "Are Becky and Rachel all right?"

"Yes, thank God," he nodded soberly. "Calvin and Mary, too . . . but the wolves got into the Wheatley house and killed Zeb, his wife and their four kids . . . and . . . and Terry Sitwell got caught out in the open. They pulled him down thirty yards from his front door."

"The bastard!" I cursed under my breath. "Terry . . . and Wheatley was the one who still thought Thatcher had stolen the Bishop child. He was right, too . . . and Thatcher's killed him."

"What d'you mean?" asked Sam confusedly.

"Nothing yet," I put him off. "You and Will get your truck and meet me at Calvin's house. Where is he, anyway?"

"Over there," said Langdon, pointing into the cemetery. "But what . . . ?"

"Just do it, Sam," I snapped at him. "I'll explain everything. I'm still having a hard time trying to believe some of the things I've seen . . . but I know what we've got to do."

He shrugged and went off to collect Will Daley. I jumped the fence and strode towards the small knot of people in the cemetery itself. Calvin was there, with the county sheriff and his men, and he rushed up to fling his arms around me when he caught sight of me.

"Goddam!" he exclaimed. "Never thought I'd see ya 'mong the livin' again! Whole town's one big disaster. I got me a few more scratches when one o' the brutes come through our livin' room winder."

"We've got to hurry, Calvin," I said impatiently. "What the hell is going on here?"

His face went white. Taking me by the arm, he led me one by one to six, gaping holes in the earth.

"Each one of 'em belonged to a Thatcher, Mr. Damon . . . and each coffin's been busted wide open. Ain't nothin' in 'em!"

The sheriff came over, curious as to who I was, but a warning glance to Calvin kept his explanation to a minimum. Then he dragged me to the rear of the cemetery, to the wrought-iron fence, and pointed. Just beyond the fence lay another heap of forest animals, ripped apart as they had been in my camp. Beside them, a set of large footprints showed in the forest mould, facing the cemetery and then retreating back the way they had come.

"There ain't no footprints in the graveyard," said

Calvin, wrinkling his nose at the all-too-familiar odour that hung over the place. "The sheriff figgers that whoever done the diggin' did it two nights ago when we was out on the ridge and the rain washed the prints away. Don't know what t'make o'them poor critters . . . but we're gonna follow them footsteps right back t'wherever they come from."

"You're coming with me, Calvin," I said, sickened by the shredded carcasses and suddenly cognizant of how they had died. "I know where those footprints will go and we've got more important things to do."

Ignoring his look of amazement, I led him out of the cemetery and soon, he and I had joined Sam and Will in the Adderley kitchen just as Mary served up coffee. It was my turn for story-telling.

"Last night, I got chased by another pack of wolves that showed up around my camp while I was salvaging what was left of it. I killed one of them there and ran from the others. They came after me, actually gave me a chance to see safety before coming in for the kill, but I had more left in me than I thought and made it . . . into Corey Thatcher's house! I killed another wolf on his doorstep, which is where I got this."

I lifted my arm with a grim smile.

"Anyway, Corey wasn't there and since the wolves

weren't about to leave, I made myself at home. You're not going to believe half of what I'm going to tell you, but I found a diary that belonged to Elias Thatcher back in 1775!"

From there, I went on to relate everything I had read in the diary, watching their faces register curiosity, revulsion and then stark horror, all in the space of a half hour. If it had not involved the deaths of Terry Sitwell, two families and a countless number of livestock, I think I might have enjoyed being the only one who knew all the answers; but playing Sherlock Holmes had not unearthed the whereabouts of Elisabeth Bishop and the possibility of what might happen to her in spite of my efforts was not comforting.

"I think Thatcher opened those graves last night," I continued. "You were right about him being crazy, Calvin . . . but he's crazy and extremely dangerous. He's the descendant of a blood-hungry ghoul and he does have some strange power over wolves because he can change himself into one at will! Thatcher left me a warning of dead animals at my campsite and he left the one outside the cemetery . . . except that I think his warnings are also the main course of his dinners nowadays."

"Come on, Mr. Damon," objected Calvin. "Yer

talkin' 'bout them werewolf movies they been showin' in the theatres."

"Don't you think I know what it sounds like, Calvin?" I said heatedly. "Don't you think I've weighed out all the things I've seen and weighed them out again just to make sure Corey Thatcher and I don't belong in the same nut-house? I'll believe anything after seeing what was left of the wolf I killed on Thatcher's porch. Besides, it would explain how the Bishop girl was kidnapped and why there were footprints in the nursery but only wolf-tracks outside."

"But what are the wolves?" asked Sam incredulously. "And why didn't all of them on the ridge turn to powder?"

"Some of the wolves were just plain wolves, Sam. The others were Elias Thatcher's crew members turned into wolves by Kerinna Thatcher in 1776 and endowed with the same vitality that allowed her to live over a hundred and twenty years . . . so long as they all had their rations of blood. Why do you think your town has been plagued by wolves for a century and a half?"

"You expect us t'believe all this, Mr. Damon?" said Calvin, shaking his head.

"Believe whatever pleases you, Calvin. Whether it's true or not, Corey Thatcher has still managed to kidnap the Bishop's baby and he intends to sacrifice her in an attempt to bring that stone idol to life. *He believes he can do it and that's all that matters now.* God knows why he dug up those graves. Maybe he thinks a few rotting corpses will help his incantations. I don't know. He's denied everything, but I'll swear he's lying through his teeth. And I'll swear he knows where this cave is and that it's somewhere on his property, too.

"At first, I couldn't make up my mind about him. He went back and forth between normality and abnormality. But this morning he came into his house shouting, "They're empty!", knowing full well that I was there all along and trying to throw me off the scent by pretending to have had nothing to do with emptying the graves of his family. He's no fool and he's out for revenge on this town before anything else. That's why we've got to find that cave before tonight. When his damned magic doesn't work, he just might get angry enough to try some with those dynamite charges as catalysts."

"Do you think maybe he's killed the girl already, Mr. Damon?" asked Will Daley.

"I doubt it. The diary entry specified that the sacrifice had to be alive. Thatcher will act accordingly."

*　　　　*　　　　*

Between us, we decided to let the rest of the townspeople lead the sheriff on a wild goose chase to the Thatcher house. Everyone still remembered Zeb Wheatley's last charge that Corey Thatcher had stolen the Bishop child. His death and that of his entire family, coupled with the fact that no one but a Thatcher would have cause to open Thatcher graves, would surely bring them up to the house again — leaving us free to look for the cave without the threat of detection that two dozen angry farmers and their families would surely cause. As unobtrusively as possible, all of us made a stop at Calvin's store for firearms, leaving Mary there to cover for us while we drove out to the Thatcher property ahead of everyone else.

Each of us carried a high-powered hunting rifle and we kept within earshot lest the wolves make another unexpected appearance. Our search dragged well on into the afternoon with no results; and though we intended to continue it in spite of the small chance of finding the mouth of a cave on two hundred acres of property, we were close to admitting defeat when we finally reached what had been my campsite. There we sat disconsolately, staring out at the hull of my submerged boat where it glinted in the bright sunlight over the lake.

"Wolves sure did a number on your stuff, too, Mr. Damon," observed Calvin. I nodded.

"It's got to be Thatcher's guiding intelligence behind them. Ordinary wolves wouldn't have come close to doing this much damage. I don't know how he does it, but he manages it quite well."

"He sure did his best t'get you outta here," said Will, surveying the ruin of my equipment. "Maybe the cave's 'round here somewhere and he wanted ya out so's ya wouldn't find it by accident."

"That could be," I agreed, "but I was through most of these woods when I first got here, looking for a place to camp before I decided on this spot. It's all mostly flatland and when I think of a cave, I see it set into a hill or something like that."

"Then yer talkin 'bout the other side o' the lake," offered Calvin, "cause the land there starts rollin' out towards the mountains. We oughta bail yer boat out and row over there if we're gonna keep lookin'; but we better hurry cause we only got three or four more hours a daylight left."

It was nearing six o'clock when we reached the opposite shore of the lake and pressed on into the woods. The undergrowth was thicker, heavier than on the other side, obviously less travelled, if at all, by anything else besides forest creatures. Our progress was slow, slower still because we were exhausted and just going through the motions in preference to admitting failure. After two hours, we were a mile or so inland, taking council in a small clearing and now ready to call ourselves quits in the face of the deepening shadows that surrounded us. We had just decided to turn back when Will uttered an exclamation of surprise and reached into a clump of bushes.

"That's my fishing rod!" I cried. "The one I lost in the lake!"

"Can't be, Mr. Damon," said Calvin. "How could it get here if ya lost it back there?" he queried, jerking a thumb behind him in the direction of the lake.

"I don't know," I answered, "but I'm sure . . . "

Suddenly, we all crouched down where we stood and looked in the direction of the sound of snapping twigs that came to us through the twilight.

"My God!" choked Sam. "What is that thing?"

Recognition and memory flashed through my brain in the same instant. Into our view came the head and shoulders of the man I had seen swimming on the lake two days before; or rather, *in* the lake, because it dawned on me that no fish could have pulled my rod out of my boat and a mile inland. Again, I felt the curious revulsion as I gazed at the bloated shape and saw the lurching gait of the man's passage through the woods. He lifted two hands, ten dough-like fingers to his mouth — and when they came away, they were smeared with the blood and fur of some small animal. I tore my gaze away in time to see Will Daley, his face etched with terror, rise and turn to run. As I pulled him down, a branch cracked beneath us and I heard Calvin's panic-stricken cry of dismay.

"It's Tobias Thatcher!"

The snapping branch had been heard by the man and he had looked around for the source of the noise. As I stared with loathing at his blotched, purple-skinned face, the lips crimsoned with blood, I heard Calvin's sickened whisper again.

"I seen a picture of him once. I know it's him . . . but he's dead. He drowned in the lake over sixty years ago."

Sam muttered a prayer and crossed himself as we crouched in stunned silence, wishing it would turn away its scabrous, peeling face and so relieve us of the shuddering nausea that crept up from our stomachs.

"And then he woke up, hooked himself on my line and dragged the whole thing out here," I whispered hoarsely. "God! Have they all woken up? Did they claw their way out of their graves and start feasting in my camp?"

"Let's get outta here, Mr. Damon," pleaded Will. "I don't care if that's Toby Thatcher or not. It's horrible. Please, let's get outta here."

The thing that was Tobias Thatcher turned and lurched away. I found Sam, Will and Calvin looking at me, waiting for a decision as if it were entirely up to me. We sat on the ground like that, uncomfortably, like children who have seen one of their worst nightmares come to life and are too scared to do anything but sit, close to tears and completely overwhelmed by their fear. I had to suppress my own desire to run when I spoke.

"We've got to follow that thing," I said slowly. "The Wheatley family is gone. Vandermeer's family is gone. Terry is gone and half the livestock in this area as well. It's getting close to nightfall now . . . Midsummer's Eve. That thing is going to the cave we're looking for . . . to join the man responsible for everything . . . and that man is going to add a two-month old baby to the casualty list."

I hardly felt like shaming three grown men into doing something even I didn't want to do; but my remarks had the desired effect. We got up, chastened for our fear, and went after the grisly thing that Calvin had named Tobias Thatcher. All the while, I was thinking that I had *witnessed* the resurrection of a corpse as it had risen up out of sixty-odd years of mud and slime on the lake bottom! And we caught up to him, smelled him, gained to a safe distance behind him and were thankful for all the meals we hadn't eaten that day.

"Make sure you've got a round in the chamber," I advised hurriedly, brandishing my own rifle. "It's getting dark and we might see some wolves awfully soon . . . but don't fire unless it means our lives and if we make it to the cave, don't make any unnecessary noise."

I was not at all reassured by the manner of my three companions and hoped that whatever chances we had of finding the cave would not be spoiled by a rash move by one of them. Our quarry was not difficult to follow, making a great deal of racket in its awkward progress through the underbrush. It stopped often, as if trying to get its bearings for a moment, and then would stumble off again into the fast-falling dusk. My only worry was that the cave was still too far away to be reached in some light. If we had to follow Tobias Thatcher in darkness, he might enter the cave without us ever seeing him do so and then we would never find the entrance.

I wondered what Calvin, Sam and Will were thinking. It could do no good for anyone's sanity to consciously admit to following a man who had died over a half century before. The absolute morbidity of it was a continual temptation within me to laugh, and as we scrambled after our quarry I was close to nervous hysteria under the pressure of keeping him in sight. He passed close to a hillside that bulged up out of the forest and I blinked as a branch swung into my face. When I looked again, he was gone!

Instinctively, we rose as one to rush to the place where we had last seen him, but I held back.

"Wait!" I cautioned. "He can't have gone anywhere but into the cave and the entrance has got to be in that hillside. Give him a few minutes, then we can find the entrance and follow. If we blunder around right away, he . . . it . . . might hear us."

As it was, I had to strike through an entire book of matches before we found the entrance — a small circle about the size of a manhole cover set into a small depression at the foot of the hill and much overgrown with weeds and briars. The four of us stood around it, breathing hard.

"This is it," I whispered, and forced myself to be the first one into the hole.

Slowly, I lowered myself waist-deep into the smudgy blackness of the hole and found my feet resting on an earthen shelf. I crouched down, slinging my rifle over one shoulder and feeling around with my hands. There was another shelf six inches down and another below that. A stairway! I looked up and saw three shapes silhouetted against a small circle of darkening sky.

"All clear," I whispered up to them. "A stairway starts a yard down from the entrance. Take it slow. One at a time."

I don't know what it was that made me take that first, awful step down. I tried to analyze the emotions that prompted me to it. It might have been the thought of those who had already died and the innocent child that was to be murdered even more callously . . . yet I had never met any of them besides Terry Sitwell and the town of Thatcher's Ferry meant nothing to me beyond being a place I had chosen at random for my vacation. I suppose, had I ever told anyone about it, they would have called it Courage; but I had never known such a thing as Courage. Never in my life had anything hinged upon whether or not I had any

Courage in me. As a medic in Germany, I was sick with fear and disgust as often as not, but I did what was expected of me because I was ordered to do so, not out of any courageous streak in my nature. I think it must have been curiosity again. I had seen something that someone I knew swore to have died years before. I had been threatened, warned away by a man who had ultimately directed a pack of wolves to bring me down; a man who was obviously insane, yet nevertheless logical and calculating. A diary filled with impossibilities had aroused my latent desire to experience something out of the ordinary . . . and I think it was jealously pitting myself against Corey Thatcher on a physical level because my life had been a boring battle of wits; because he was a giant of a man whereas I was only a man; because he had challenged me, made open mockery of my attempts to thwart him . . . and I was curious to see where it was all to end. In any case, when I saw the three faces still outlined above me, I added anger to my list of incentives.

"Goddamit!" I hissed. "I'm not gonna do this by myself. If at least one of you doesn't get down here in the next ten seconds, I'm coming back up and Thatcher can screw your damn town into the ground!"

"There's wolves comin' up behind us, Mr. Damon," whined Will Daley. "If we hurry, we can still make a run for it."

"No!" I almost shouted. "You stupid hicks! It's safer down here now. Can't you see this whole thing started a hundred and seventy years ago; that Thatcher means to ruin your town? It was your ancestours who burned Elias Thatcher. At least they had the guts to fight back against him. If you don't help me to end it here and now, you can kiss everything you've ever known good-bye . . . and probably before you can make it back to town. The wolves alone could do it. And if Corey Thatcher knows more than we've given him credit for, it could be a lot worse."

They knew I was talking about the stone idol. It didn't matter that we had no proof of its actual existence. My inference to their cowardice, the threat of the unknown and the wolves drawing nearer were enough to overcome their reluctance. In a few minutes, they were beside me on the stairway and I had lit one match for an initial reconnoitering of our position. The steps descended another twenty feet or so into a low, broad passageway of stone that twisted off into the darkness beyond the glow of my match. I drew a deep breath as I glimpsed the faces around me, deciding that scared company was better than no company at all.

"All right," I said, drawing them closer. "No sounds. Nothing, not if you can help it. I'll go first.

You can all follow by holding on to the belt of whoever's in front of you. Don't even think of using rifles unless we've got no other chance of getting out of here."

The match flickered out, leaving us no light but the small circle of emerging stars above. That, too, disappeared as we started off down the stairs and into the passageway below. The darkness became so complete that we might just as well have been blind for all the purpose our eyes served.

I edged along one wall of the tunnel, feeling my way on its cold, clammy surface. In some spots it was wet and slimed with moss-like growths that we were probably lucky not to see. I could not judge distances, but our snail-like progress seemed to encompass the years of a lifetime and as the tomb-like atmosphere began to grow oppressive, I caught faint snatches of prayer from Sam Langdon and whimpers of fear from Will Daley. It was odd not to hear Calvin's incessant chatter, but he had not said a word since finding the cave. I reasoned that if he was feeling half as afraid as I was, then he was more than likely too scared to bother with speech.

The tunnel started to slope downwards, gently at first, but then more steeply until we were leaning back on our heels as we walked, trying to keep our feet on a floor that had also grown slippery with water and slime. Up until then, we had not made much in the way of noise beyond our laboured breathing. Now there were hurried shufflings and the dull thud of rifle butts being used to steady our faltering steps.

"We gotta go back," came an hysterical whisper.

"Be quiet, Will," I said as kindly as possible. "We don't have any choice but to go on."

The tunnel levelled out abruptly and my foot struck something that rattled in the Stygian blackness. I almost panicked when, in kneeling, I felt a long smooth shape that was knobbed at both ends. I reached further and found others like it and then a large, rounded shape. I said nothing, steeling myself to walk cross-wise into emptiness, hoping to find the other wall before the others realized what I was doing. I knew I had stumbled into at least a pair of skeletons lying in the darkness.

"I'm crossing to the other wall," I said in response to an intuitive feeling of protest behind me. "Never mind why. Don't panic. Here it is now."

Inwardly, I sighed with relief. Not a word had been spoken by anyone. If not for the hand on my belt, it would have felt as if I were walking alone; but the rough surface of the wall against my hand again was reassuring. The passage plunged downwards a second time and I guessed that we had gone well over a hundred feet down into the earth. I noticed, too, that the air was becoming thick with a peculiar odour. It was incense, but of some hellish concoction that was both suffocating and sweet with evil. I sensed that we were coming closer to the final confrontation with Corey Thatcher and slowed our pace. The tunnel bent sharply to the left, back again to the right, and suddenly the underground cavern yawned in front of us, filled with a blazing, smoke-ridden light.

As our eyes became accustomed once again to light, the immensity of the chamber grew apparent. It was a natural bubble in solid rock, fully sixty feet from floor to cragged ceiling, roughly circular with a diameter nearing seventy-five yards. Standing braziers of dully gleaming metal lit the entire place, spewing also the acrid smell of incense into the air. At the flat end of the chamber, two of them flanked an altar of stone . . . and behind the altar, the Ancient One!

The idol was nearly as tall as the cavern itself, carved from some black, lustreless tone that showed numerous cracks as I gazed up along its full height. It was hewn in the likeness of something mid-way between a man and a beast — a giant anthropomorph with

taloned hands and feet, sculptured into a muscular development that was awesome with suggestive power and hideously crowned, not with a human head, but with the furred, snarling snout of a wolf! Its eyes were two gleaming jewels of topaz and I felt drawn to them, mesmerized by the flicker and play of the brazier fires in their translucent depths.

We stepped out onto the floor of the cavern, over symbols and figures carved into the stone. I discerned another passage leading off from the chamber about thirty feet to the right of the altar. We edged closer, craning our necks to look up at the mammoth figure of stone that dwarfed us.

"It's real," I breathed. "All the way from Persia and they carried it down here, piece by piece."

That we had come thus far to meet an enemy on his own ground suddenly ceased to have any meaning as we stared at the giant man-wolf of stone. A tangible force descended upon us, crushing us down to our knees. A voice seemed to whisper promises of ever-lasting life. It filled the spirit with visions of power, an uplifting beyond the ordinary strivings of mere men. It radiated that promise, teasing us with it, flaunting it as within our grasp . . . but beneath it I felt the malice and the evil. I saw the promise for the slavery that it was. Almost too late, I heard the chanting that had begun to fill the chamber and I saw Calvin, Will and Sam on their knees beside me, their faces a heart-breaking mixture of acceptance and pitiful, struggling defiance. Wildly, I scanned the walls for some place of concealment, but we had no choices. The idol itself would have to hide us from our enemies!

The chanting grew louder as I dragged my dazed and bewildered companions behind the splayed talons of the idol's feet. Trembling, I crept back around to see what would issue from the passage on the other side of the altar . . . And the stone moved! It writhed and quivered beneath my touch . . . as if in anticipation! Its towering bulk was a sentient mountain of horror waiting to be brought to total life . . . and out from the passage came the first of the grisly things that had been the Thatcher family!

The blue coat of Captain Elias Thatcher was covered with patches of fungus and mouldering rot, the brass buttons almost black with age. What remained of his face was a seared, pustulant chaos of misplaced, flame-wracked features surrounded by straggling wisps of beard and hair. His eyes were alive, but with an infernal light that was unholy by its very brightness. In his skeletal hands he carried a naked infant, Elisabeth

Bishop, and his cracked and twisted lips moved soundlessly in the words of his chant.

Behind him limped a dark-haired woman whose pale skin and the gaping wound in her throat proclaimed her to be Sarah Patterson. Beside her was a man with a ragged wound above his heart and a face that, in life, had been twisted with madness — Amory Thatcher. There was, too, the tumescent figure of Tobias, his ghastly, blood-smeared face more swollen and livid in the firelight than it had been aboveground. At his side, naked, was the drooling, blank-faced Amy Tanner, her belly sagged and swollen down over her spindly thighs. Behind them were two ragged creatures in the final stages of natural corruption that clung to each other, pathetically, as they walked. The broken shaft of an arrow protruded from the skull of one, the ill-fated Jeremiah. The other I took to be a woman, though who she might have been I could not guess. And following them, the last in that hideous procession, was a tall, slender woman who moved sinuously in the wake of horror. Her paste-white flesh was unblemished, her eyes quick and bright with a life far superior to the "undead" who shambled before her. Triumphantly she moved to the head of the procession, joining the lich of Elias Thatcher, taking his arm to lead him to the altar. Somehow, it was Kerinna Thatcher reborn again!

"Where's Corey?" whispered a voice directly behind me. I turned and found Calvin peering anxiously over my shoulder.

"I don't know. How are Will and Sam?"

"Okay. You think Lissie Bishop's still alive?"

"I think she has to be alive, according to their ritual," I answered him.

Kerinna Thatcher's chanting rose in a monotonous litany that filled the caver as the liches of the Thatcher family formed a semicircle around the altar. Elias laid the unmoving baby on the bare stone and then raised his fleshless hands upward to the idol. The chanting ceased, and Kerinna's voice echoed through the chamber as her eyes flamed with fiendish exultation.

"Ancient One, Ye Who art not to be named, behold ye the uplifted faces of thine own flock. Behold thee thy son, my husband Elias. Behold thee thine own Amory and Tobias and Amy. Behold thee thy children Sarah and Jeremiah and fair Catherine whom we have brought to thee from her shallow rest in far Massachusetts Bay. Behold thee all of us who wouldst call thee 'Master' and be forever in service to thee. Look ye upon this girl-child whom we shall despoil of Life,

Soul and Spirit that Ye mayst walk upon this earth in
Thy might and splendour!"

We watched as Sarah Patterson moved towards
the Captain, a mirthless grin upon her pallid lips that
was every bit as terrible as the crusted, worm-eaten
slash in her throat. From a small, leathern bag at her
side she drew out a golden sickle and three small
bowls, setting them on the altar beside the child.

"I thought Corey was runnin the show, Mr.
Damon," said Calvin, and then I heard his voice shaken
with dismay. "My God, would ya listen t'me? Here I
am lookin' at walkin' corpses like it happens every
day . . . "

His voice became tinged with hysteria and I turned
to him quickly, taking him by the shoulders.

"I thought Corey would be here by now," I whispered, shaking him violently. "But we can't wait anymore. Tell Sam and Will that when I make a run for
the baby, you hit those things with everything you've
got and then run like hell for the passageway."

Calvin nodded dumbly and turned away. Meanwhile, Kerinna had stepped forward, raising the golden
sickle and murmuring words from another language.
I crouched for the leap that would take me to the altar
. . . and another voice boomed through the cavern.

"STOP! THIS FAMILY WILL NO LONGER BEAR THE CURSE OF YOUR LUST AND BLAS-PHEMY!"

Corwin Thatcher was running across the cavern towards the altar with his shotgun in one hand and a knapsack slung over one shoulder. Elias shuddered where he stood beside Kerinna, displeasure registering on the putrid flesh of his face. Kerinna whirled around, her eyes ablaze with a feral light of hatred. She pointed, and Tobias and Amory went to meet the last living member of their family. Then she faced the altar again and began to intone:

"O Ancient One, Father of the Black Wind that tramples down the Light, accept thee the blood of this girl-child . . . "

"NOW!" I shouted, and fired a bullet into the forehead of the she-witch at the altar, staggering her back from her victim. Calvin, Sam and Will began their barrage as I raced for the child and above the din, I heard Corey Thatcher's bellowing.

"Damon, you fool! The wolves are behind me!"

As I reached the altar, Elias Thatcher loomed above me with his skeletal hands reaching for my throat. My rifle exploded in his face, shattering the brittle bone and ragged flesh into total ruin. Eluding his grasp, I swung the rifle hard against what was left of his head, battering the bloodless body into a splintered heap beneath the altar. And from the mouth of the passageway from whence we had come, came the howling rush of grey wolves.

Within seconds, the cavern had become a scene of frenzied chaos, the air filled with the sweet suffocation of incense and the stench of the grave. As the wolves swarmed out over the chamber floor, Corey rushed into the arms of Tobias and Amory, screaming in a berserk fury. My rifle spat fire as I squeezed off shot after shot into the snarling wall of grey fur that loped towards us. Sam dashed to Thatcher's aid, clubbing Amory to the stone floor and narrowly avoiding the lunge of a wolf by falling to the ground beside the mouldering corpse. Corey jammed his shotgun into Tobias's stomach, discharging both barrels at once and exploding the bloated body into a thousand, slithering tatters of flesh.

"Get out,Damon!" he roared, but our escape was barred by the wolves and I stood my ground before the altar as Corey disappeared under a bristling mountain of grey-furred bodies.

Then, like a Titan, he staggered up and forward, slamming his shotgun against Sarah Patterson's head and all but tearing it from her shoulders even as her fingers raked across his face. Calvin and Will had riddled the pathetic bodies of Jeremiah, Catherine Fletcher and Amy Tanner to the ground and retreated back towards me. Sam joined us a moment later and we began firing blindly into the press of wolves that milled around us.

Some inner prescience warned me; or perhaps, it was a faint prickling of my skin that alerted me to the danger at my back. When I turned, it was to face the tall, black-robbed figure of Kerinna Thatcher, a bullet hole between her eyes oozing blood and the golden sickle in her hand already descending on a course that would bury it in my chest. I swung my rifle instinctively, knocking the blade aside, and all Time seemed to stand still. The clamour faded from my ears as I faced the she-witch, shrank from the unspeakable hatred darting from her blood-rimmed eyes like poisoned barbs. Again, my rifle thundered . . . and suddenly the witch was no longer an easy mark at point-blank range but a monstrous black wolf in mid-air, leaping for my throat!

As I hit the stone floor, naught but my unflung rifle stayed its fangs from my throat. My head began to spin dizzily, a roaring filled my ears and then I

realized it was Corey Thatcher, shouting as he wrenched
the wolf high into the air above his head and dashed it
down again at his feet. Dazedly, I struggled up . . . and
found myself facing two Corey Thatchers!

"Run, Damon," panted one of them.

"Kill it, Damon," panted the other. The barrel of
my rifle wavered.

"A shapeshifter, Damon . . . looks like me . . . I'm
Corey Thatcher . . . "

"No. I'm Corey Thatcher. Shoot him . . . "

An agony of indecision vanished with those words.
I looked first to one and then to the other of the two
beings claiming to be Corey Thatcher. Both wore the
rags of a flannel shirt and denims, both faces oozed
tiny rills of blood, both had knapsacks dangling from
one shoulder . . . but one of them had said, "I'm Corey
Thatcher. Shoot *him* . . . ", and that one's eyes were
kindled with crimson-flecked fires straight from Hell
Itself. My fingers curled around the trigger of the
rifle and pulled hard . . . The cavern trembled at the
shriek of infernal rage and frustration that staggered
me backwards and crowded all other sound from my
ears. When I looked up again, Corey Thatcher, the
real Corey Thatcher, was grappling with the black
wolf!

"Run, Damon!" he roared. "For God's sakes, man, grab the baby and get out of here!"

I stumbled to the altar where Sam, Will and Calvin still fired on the rapidly decreasing number of wolves that snapped around them. Dropping my rifle, I scooped up the small, inert bundle that was Elisabeth Bishop and began to run for the entrance to the passage-way.

"Thatcher!" I yelled. "Come on, we've got the baby!"

It was only when the four of us had reached the mouth of the tunnel that I handed Elisabeth to Calvin and looked back. Corey stood over a black wolf that snarled angrily where it lay on the floor, its forepaws clawing the stone, dragging its useless hind-quarters behind. He reeled away from the beast, reaching into his pack with one hand as he wiped a welter of blood from his face with the other.

"Thatcher!" I cried. "It's done. Come on."

"Go! I'll follow you . . . "

In his hand was a stick of dynamite that he lit at one of the braziers beside the altar. The fuse sputtered and flared as Corey flung it to the feet of the black colossus rising above him. He spun around, two more sticks of explosive alight in his hands as he ran towards me. Sam, Calvin and Will took off into the tunnel as the first explosion rocked the cavern. The idol trembled, groaned sideways and began to tumble. Corey flung away the sticks of dynamite, lit another pair and flung them away. Too late, I saw the squirming shape of the black wolf waver and change. Too late, I saw the crimson eyes of Kerinna Thatcher fall upon the golden sickle near her right hand, snatch it up and hurl it into the back of her great-great-grandson. Corey stumbled and fell against a brazier, spilling liquid fire in ever-widening pools across the floor of the cavern.

"Thatcher!" I cried, starting towards him. He looked up at me, smiled, and waved back.

"Go, Damon. This is all I deserve . . . for what they have done before me."

The fires leapt up around him but he made no sound. The cavern thundered, fireballed with a dozen explosions and a high, piercing scream came through it all. I stumbled into the double twist of the tunnel as the ceiling and idol of the Ancient One crumbled down on Kerinna, the Thatchers, the wolves . . . and Corey.

EPILOGUE

Ages later, I staggered up against Calvin where he, Will and Sam huddled at the foot of an earthen stairway beneath a starry circle of sky. Elisabeth Bishop had awakened from her no doubt drug-induced slumber and wrapped in Sam Langdon's shirt, cooed softly in contentment. The moon shone brightly down on a densely wooded landscape — and a shallow depression where a hill used to be — that was curiously silent after the reverberations that had swept over me in the tunnel. None of us said very much on the way back to town, not even Calvin. The closest he came to his normal self was one incredulous observation as we rowed back across the lake.

"Who woulda thought it o' mad Corey Thatcher? Looks like he was takin' care of us all along . . . "

*   *   *

I go back to Thatcher's Ferry every year on my vacation — to fish, relax, to see Calvin Adderley and Sam and Will. Calvin has an extra chapter for his story but I don't think he'll ever tell it to anyone. It's become

170

a ritual of sorts for the four of us, though. When mid-June rolls around, they all know I'll be coming soon and they wait for me. I bring gifts for Becky Langdon and Lissie Bishop. Mary Adderley, Rachel Langdon and Myra Bishop all have their best tablecloths out airing for a week before I'm expected, already having decided what they'll serve when they invite me to dinner. I tell Stan and Myra that it was Corey Thatcher who saved their baby from the wolves. They don't believe me . . . but it's like I've become "country folk" to them even though I spend fifty weeks in every year being "city folk."

For most of the time that I'm there, Calvin, Will, Sam and I try to pretend like it was something warm and good that forged the bonds of Friendship — but each of us knows the real reason why I come back year after year. It was better when Corey Thatcher was alive. At least then we could see him and know that he lived and breathed like the rest of us . . . and though we feel a kinship now, the four of us who saw the cavern and the idol, we know it's really a common fear that binds our lives together. And when Midsummer's Eve comes, we all take a long walk out from town, to the Thatcher property and around the lake to where a small circular hole in the earth still gapes wide at the foot of a hill that isn't there anymore. We won't go down there again, ever . . . but we spend the night around that hole and wonder if Corey Thatcher can do in Death what he did in Life — or if we'll see him again someday, along with the wolves and the rest of the Thatchers, trailing behind a giant wolf of stone come to life from under the earth.

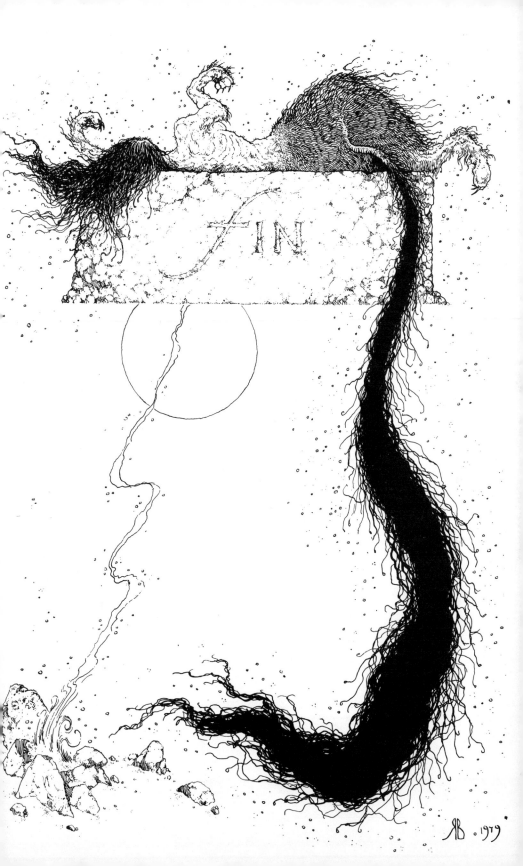